**"We ag̲̅___ ___ ___ ___ ___ ___ ___ ___
me, rem___ ___**

She worried her lips, studying him.

"Seriously, Rainey, I apparently need some help, and trust me, it takes a lot for me to admit that. I'm more of a work-hard-and-you'll-achieve-your-goal kind of a guy, but this parenting thing doesn't come with a playbook." Scott grabbed at the base of his head, hating the tension that attacked him. This wasn't him.

"Henry needs you to be firm. I'm guessing y'all were more like buddies when you were just his fun uncle. Then you could buy him ice cream and doughnuts and let him stay up late with you playing video games." She gestured in the direction of the television like it was a crate of processed food.

"I thought he needed time to heal and get used to me."

"You might be right, but he doesn't have any problem obeying me."

"I've noticed."

"I know you're used to winning, and I'm sure you hate it as much as I do when people repeat that saying about it being how you play the game that matters, but this isn't a game, and it does matter how you play. For what it's worth, and I get it that I'm not much of an authority, but I think you're doing your best."

Award-winning author **Leslie DeVooght** writes women's fiction with faith, love, laughter and a lot of Southern charm. When Leslie isn't writing, she's cheering on her three children and enjoying date nights with her husband, who loves that she researches kissing. In addition to her own stories, Leslie co-owns *Spark Flash Fiction*, an online magazine that publishes short, short romance collections. Join Leslie's newsletter at lesliedevooght.com to receive her free book, *If Only*.

Books by Leslie DeVooght

Love Inspired

Taking a Second Shot

Visit the Author Profile page at LoveInspired.com.

TAKING A
SECOND SHOT

LESLIE DeVOOGHT

LOVE INSPIRED
INSPIRATIONAL ROMANCE

ISBN-13: 978-1-335-62135-1

Taking a Second Shot

Recycling programs
for this product may
not exist in your area.

Love Inspired
22 Adelaide St. West, 41st Floor
Toronto, Ontario M5H 4E3, Canada
www.LoveInspired.com

HarperCollins Publishers
Macken House, 39/40 Mayor Street Upper,
Dublin 1, D01 C9W8, Ireland
www.HarperCollins.com

Printed in Lithuania

I press toward the mark for the prize of
the high calling of God in Christ Jesus.
—*Philippians* 3:14

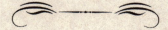

For Charlie, my Bug, the Chili Con Queso. You will always be my favorite player! May you always run in such a way to win the most important prize.

Chapter One

Rainey Allen punched in the code on the school security keypad, dodging the nerves attacking her like defenders on the soccer field. She'd never allowed anxiety to stop her on the pitch, and she wouldn't let it tie her in knots today. Even if this place had witnessed the worst time of her life, she was no longer an awkward preteen girl. She was a strong woman, and she refused to miss her strength-training session.

Squaring her shoulders, she strode into the nearly empty high school. Too bad it was also home to the middle school. More specifically, the gym, the scene of her unfortunate square-dance fiasco. Usually, the memory was locked tightly away in a mental fortress rivaling a supermax prison, but when the beast managed to escape, it breathed fire over her and coiled tightly around her stomach.

If there'd been another option, she'd have taken it, but in the small town of Woodley, Georgia, the school was the only place with a weight room, and it doubled as the PE coach's office. Since her grandfather served as both a local pastor and the chair of the school board, he'd given her permission to use the space. As the weight-room door clicked shut, Rainey swiped the beads of sweat lined up along her hairline. The coach's desk was covered in papers. What a mess. He needed to get organized before he missed something important.

After pulling off her sweatshirt, she navigated the single row of weight benches and dropped her bag on the floor beside a few chairs facing a wall-mounted television. She tossed her sweatshirt on a chair and surveyed the room. A metal shelf held a few sets of hand weights. Near the benches, racked barbells rested on basic stands, and stacks of weighted plates sat under one of the benches. Other equipment was scattered about the room in cubbies and tubs. It wasn't as bad as she'd expected, but far from her normal workout facilities.

The pungent scent of citrus disinfectant stung her nostrils, but it was better than the alternative aroma of body odor. While not well organized, at least she knew the equipment was clean and the familiar scent brought her a measure of comfort, reminding her of all the gyms where she'd trained. Even though it lacked the best equipment, when she used precise form, she wouldn't need high-tech machines.

Rainey massaged her hamstring, still tender but healing and growing stronger. After weeks working with her trainer, she could continue her recovery on her own. Rainey found an exercise band in the bottom of a tub and a bench to use for her necessary hamstring curls. She secured one end of the band around the leg of the power tower and placed her ankles in the loops at the band's other end before lying on her stomach on the narrow bench. With her hands pressed firmly on the floor, she contracted her hamstrings to curl her heels toward her seat.

"One." She clamped her eyes closed and held the position, letting her muscles quiver before she slowly straightened her legs. Who needed top-of-the-line equipment with knowledge and ingenuity on their side? She took controlled breaths as she repeated the move. *Excellent.*

If nothing else, her teammates and coaches praised her technique. She just needed to make it all come together on the soccer field. Squeezing her eyes shut, she contracted the muscles again. "Five." She exhaled slowly, lowering her feet to the resting position for a few seconds before continuing the exercise.

Focus on the results. See the goal. No distractions.

The twang of a banjo followed by the squeal of a fiddle erupted and blasted through the room, setting the memory beast free. With a fierce intensity, dread yanked her legs rigid against the bench and grasped her lungs. Rainey struggled to gain control, but the monster fought with flaming arrows, engulfing her body.

No distractions!

"Bow to your partner." From the television's speaker, a man's voice called over the noise she refused to classify as music.

Rainey wrapped her arms around her head and clasped her hands. Nothing would stop her recovery. With a deep exhale, she curled her legs.

Someone tapped her shoulder near the edge of her tank. "As much as I hate to interrupt such a *unique* workout, who exactly are you?"

Rainey whipped her head up to meet dark brown eyes under the brim of a baseball hat. She gasped, dropping her feet. No, it couldn't be him. After a long, slow blink, she peeked again, but he was still there—Scott Wilcox, her middle-school square-dance partner.

And now, he had the nerve to cock a brow and give her that sly, lopsided grin. "Well, I'll be—" He shook his head. "If it ain't Rainey 'The Dancing Queen' Allen."

"Swing your girl. Promenade. 'til you get back home," the square-dance caller hollered.

Annoyance prickled Rainey's nerves, producing pellets of sweat along her spine. Time to make her escape. She slapped the sides of the bench and thrust herself up, but her ankles tangled in the exercise band and forced her down. She grabbed for the bench, but her sweaty palms slipped as she fell sideways.

"Whoa." Scott caught her before she hit the floor and steadied her on the bench. "Probably need to take this off before you hurt yourself." He removed the band from her ankles. "Although if you slammed into the floor, we'd be about even."

So much for him forgetting their little spin around the school gym fifteen years ago. But since it'd concluded with his arm in a cast, his forgetting was wishful thinking. Hopefully, the mishap hadn't ended his baseball career. From what she remembered, Scott and his twin brother had been described as the dynamic duo of the ball team.

"Thanks. Would you mind turning that off?" She stood and pointed at the television.

"Not planning to give square dancing another go?" Scott pulled the remote from his pocket and turned off the television. "So to what do I owe the pleasure of this little reunion?" He crossed his muscled arms over his chest and peered at her from what had to be a six-three frame. Not many men looked down at her, with her height at five feet ten inches. At least his arm seemed to have healed nicely.

"I'm visiting my grandparents for a couple of months, but I still need to train for next season." Rainey lifted the bottle filled with her special sports drink and took a gulp. If there'd been another option, she'd have taken it. But with her meager savings, her mom's condo rented and her dad's most recent fling, her grandparents' house was her only choice. Since her fledgling soccer career rarely allowed her to stay in one city longer than a season, she'd never gotten her own place.

"Next season of what?" Scott asked.

"Soccer." Rainey adjusted her headband and slid her hands

to lift her ponytail off her sticky neck. "My granddad said it would be fine for me to use the weight room. He said he sent *Coach* an email."

"He probably did." Scott shrugged.

"So if you give me your schedule, I'll work with it. It shouldn't interfere with baseball."

"Hold on." He raised a hand. "Why would you need a baseball field for soccer?"

"Well, obviously, I can't use the football field that is being overhauled. Grandpa said they hope to have it ready for the football team to condition. The outfield isn't ideal, but it'll be fine."

"Well, obviously, it won't be fine. I barely have a free minute. I can't be moving goals or coordinating schedules. Currently, I'm trying to learn the basics of the square dance in the spare seconds I have," Scott ripped off his ball cap, leaving his dark hair pressed against his head. "I'm sure your granddad didn't understand that this won't work with our conditioning in full swing and the high-school baseball season beginning in a few weeks." He gestured to a multi-month wall calendar with various school names written on dates starting in February. "Besides maintenance keeps up the field during the school day, and some of the players use it for extra practices before school and during the lunch periods. Still, you can use the weight room, just stay out of my guys' way. They don't need the distraction of a long-legged woman that looks like—like…" He rubbed his trimmed beard.

As the old waves of insecurity swirled in her stomach, Rainey resisted the urge to put on her oversize sweatshirt. How had one comment sent her back fifteen years to that gangly preteen girl all alone in the world?

"Like an athlete." Scott settled his hat on his head. "Anyway, I'm sure Pastor can find you somewhere else to kick a ball around. There's plenty of pastures and abandoned fields."

Rainey choked on her drink. "I—I can't." She coughed again. It was time to stand up for herself, no matter how much her stomach churned. Maybe this wasn't her last chance, but it certainly was her last good chance, and she wouldn't have this mammoth baseball player do anything to jeopardize her dreams of playing on a team in the National Women's Soccer League. With the side of her hand, she wiped her mouth and leveled her gaze on her old dance partner and new rival. "I will be using that field."

"We'll see about that. Once I explain the situation to your granddad, I'm sure he'll understand." Scott retrieved a set of keys from his pocket and tossed them in the air.

"Not if I get to the church first." Rainey snatched her sweatshirt and dashed out of the school. While her long legs may have seemed like a problem when she was eleven, at twenty-six, they gave her an advantage. Laughing, she sprinted across the field that connected the high school with the church grounds. No doubt, he'd need to drive to beat her.

Scott caught the door before it shut and hurried outside, but the sight of Rainey slowed his progress. *An athlete?* Had he really used that word to describe this svelte woman that ran with the grace of a gazelle? *Athlete* may have been accurate, but it failed to describe Rainey adequately. Her blond ponytail floated behind her in contrast to her sun-kissed skin, which showed the amount of time she must spend on the field, but it couldn't be his field. His heart beat hard and fast. She was sensory overload on his sleep-deprived, emotionally torn body, and that was all. It had to be. He wasn't a twelve-year-old with a crush.

At least she hadn't seen through his claim that she might distract his guys. Meanwhile, he stared after her like a benched player who was hoping to get in the game. Now, she had a head start. Groaning, he pivoted and jogged to his old jeep. The engine roared, and with a quick survey of the nearly empty parking lot, he reversed and sped to the church. He'd have to hurry to make it back in time for the team meeting before practice. With an eye on the speedometer, Scott drove around the block as fast as was allowed by law. The last thing he needed was to get stopped by Sheriff Harvey. Who would've guessed the biggest prankster in high school would now be in charge of enforcing the law?

At the front of the church, he spun the jeep into a spot and raced to the front office. Hopefully, Mrs. Ellen—his elementary-school music teacher and the church secretary, not to mention Rainey's grandmother—would be too busy to talk, but as he yanked open the door, she was standing there with hands plunked on hips, toe tapping.

"What's got you in such a hurry?" Mrs. Ellen gave him that teacher glower that never failed to keep little boys and grown men in line.

"Just wanted to chat with Pastor before ball practice."

"He's gone out back to play with the children in the extended-care program." She nodded as concern pinched her eyebrows together. "Is everything okay with Henry? He seems so withdrawn."

"We're still finding our way, but I think he's fine." Except for that he barely ate and never wanted to play catch or even video games. Scott's chest tightened as he moved to the door that led to the breezeway. He just needed to work harder. He owed it to Henry, because if it hadn't been for Scott, the little boy would still have his parents.

"We're praying for you both. You let me know if you need anything."

"Yes, ma'am." If only she could teach him how to be Henry's dad, like she'd taught him to play the xylophone in the third grade, but people in this town saw him as a hero, not the fumbling father he apparently was.

Scott might not know how to be a dad, but he did know how to coach baseball, and sharing the field with a soccer player who made his stomach quiver wasn't in his manual. He needed to hurry before Rainey convinced her grandfather that Scott was being unreasonable. At the pace she was moving, she'd surely made it to the playground. Scott turned the doorknob and stepped out.

"I know your parents are a huge help, but I'd be happy to watch Henry if you ever need a break. He's such a sweet boy."

"Yes, ma'am. Thank you." Safely through the doorway, Scott released the handle, but the door didn't click closed.

"We certainly hope to see you at church this Sunday." Mrs. Ellen held the door, smiling. "Rainey, our granddaughter, is visiting. Y'all were in school together that year she lived with us."

"Yes, ma'am. I remember her." As heat slipped up his neck, he retreated down the walkway. His mother would kill him if he acted rude to Mrs. Ellen, but he needed to stop Rainey's pleas. He was already fighting an uphill battle. What grandfather was likely to refuse his granddaughter's request, especially one that rarely visited?

"Wonderful. We'll all have to get together sometime soon."

"Yes, ma'am—that'd be nice." He bumped into the playground gate.

"Honey, you need to watch where you're going." She chuckled. "See you Sunday."

Scott snatched open the gate and darted through it.

As the gate clanged shut, Pastor Tim approached. "Scott, good to see you."

Where was Rainey? Scott scanned the area. Had he really beaten her?

"Good to see you, too, Pastor." Scott shook the older man's hand and tried to contain his excitement. But the corners of his lips stretched into what probably resembled a greedy grin. It was always more fun to win—didn't matter the competition.

"What's got you so happy?" Pastor tilted his head.

"Just enjoying this springlike day and looking forward to practicing with the guys."

"Think y'all will make it to State this year?"

"I sure hope so, but, sir, I need to talk to you about—" Out of the corner of his eye, he saw a soccer ball rolling toward him with Henry close behind and— "Rainey?"

"She told me y'all bumped into each other. Seems Henry has really taken to her and soccer. They've been passing the ball since she got here a few minutes ago."

"Hi, Uncle Scott." Henry waved and kicked the ball to Rainey. "This is my new friend, Rainey. She's Pastor Tim's granddaughter, and she plays soccer like you played baseball."

Played. The weight of regret landed on Scott's chest, heavy, solid and, most of all, permanent.

"Hi, Scott." Rainey smiled sweetly and had the nerve to bat her lashes over those slate-blue eyes as she tapped the ball to Henry.

A wave of excitement rippled over the regret. "Hi." Scott switched his attention to Pastor Tim. "Pastor, as chairman of the school board, I need to ask you to respect the high-school team's need to have priority for the baseball field. I know Rainey needs to train, and I'm happy to help her find somewhere else, but with three teams between the middle school, JV and varsity, we are already stretched thin for space."

"I hear you—"

Henry tugged on Scott's wrist. "Uncle Scott, can I play soccer?"

"What about T-ball? Like your dad and me." He ruffled

the boy's hair, which covered his ears and eyes. He needed a haircut. When had that happened? How often did five-year-olds get their hair cut, and where did they go? He'd have to check with Mom. She'd taken him for his last haircut before the funeral.

"I want to play soccer. I love it." Henry shot the ball to Rainey. "Please let me play."

"That's a fantastic idea." Pastor Tim crouched to eye level with Henry. "Coach Rainey could put together an after-school clinic."

"I'm not a coach, Grandpa, and besides I'll only be here a few weeks. Not to mention, where would we hold a clinic?" Rainey shot Scott a smug look.

"Please, Coach Rainey." Henry's bottom lip trembled. "I want to play soccer."

Scott's heart squeezed. Nothing he did with Henry was ever right, and if soccer with Rainey gave him the chance to connect with Henry, then Scott would swallow his pride and let her win. He raised his hands in defeat. "What if I was the assistant coach? You teach me the game, and when you leave, I'll take over and coach the team. We can use a part of the outfield. I'll just need to rework the schedule." If he stayed up late and got up early, he could find more time. It's not like he slept much anyway.

"Yeah!" Henry ran to Rainey and wrapped his arms around her hips.

"Really?" Rainey stared at him, her eyebrows inching up as she hugged Henry. Clearly, she'd thought he'd refuse, but she'd overplayed her hand. Although now they were stuck together, playing, of all things, soccer.

Scott rocked on his heels, fighting his urge to spare her a smirk. "I've got to get to practice. We can figure out the details tomorrow. I assume you'll be at the weight room at the same time."

"If that's okay. Scott, I really don't want to be in your way, but I need to train." She unwound Henry from her hips. "Please understand."

"Not a problem. I'm happy to help. See you tomorrow." He clapped Henry on the shoulder. "See you later, little man."

"Later, alligator." Henry didn't even glance at him. "Coach Rainey, can we keep playing?"

"'Bye, Pastor." Scott strode to the gate. What more could he do for Henry? Surely, this soccer thing would be a win for them. It had to be.

Apprehension quivered in Rainey's stomach as Scott left the play area. What was his game? His compromise had caught her off guard. She kicked the ball to Henry. "Why don't you find a couple more friends that want to play with us?"

"Yeah." Henry scooped up the ball and ran across the playground.

"I'm glad he's excited." Rainey joined her grandfather on the bench. "I hope Scott isn't too disappointed. I'm surprised he gave up so easily."

"I think Scott's struggling with his new life." Grandpa patted his knees.

"New life?"

"I prefer not to share other people's stories, but since you'll be working with Scott, and he isn't one to ask for help, I better fill you in."

"Okay." A lump formed in her belly.

"After college, the Miami Marlins drafted Scott, and he's been playing on their minor league teams ever since, working his way up in the club." Grandpa's gaze drifted to the baseball diamond in the distance. "About six months ago, he got called up from the Pensacola Blue Wahoos to play with the Jacksonville Jumbo Shrimp. It's the Marlins' triple A team."

"That's great. He probably understands where I'm coming from. But why is he here? Did he get hurt? I can't believe he'd leave a professional team to coach at a small-town high school."

"That's the hard part. It wasn't his choice." Rainey's grandpa clasped his hands. "You might remember Scott had an identical twin brother, Hank. Well, Hank married his college sweetheart, Kristen, and they moved here and had Henry a year later."

"I remember getting them confused at first, but they behaved differently. Even at twelve, Scott was confident and charismatic and fairly cocky. Hank seemed more thoughtful and happier to hang in Scott's shadow."

"Hank was always Scott's biggest supporter, so when Scott made the jump to the triple A team, Hank wanted to be in the stands when Scott took the field for the first time." Grandpa rocked forward and rested his forearms on his legs. "On the way to Jacksonville, a drunk driver collided with Hank and Kristen's car. All three were killed on impact."

"Oh, no." Rainey covered her mouth, sorrow landing within her. Poor Henry. That sweet little boy losing both his parents in an instant.

"It really rocked the town. Hank was the varsity baseball coach and the middle and high-school PE teacher. The kids loved him. Everyone loved him. Kristen worked from home, so she was able to spend lots of time with Henry. This is the most carefree I've seen Henry since the accident. I'm sure everyone and everything reminds him of his parents."

"But I'm new and soccer is new." Rainey spotted Henry passing the ball with a couple of children. "This suddenly feels like a lot of pressure. What if I mess him up more?" She rubbed her middle as the weight of her words settled inside her. She was not up to this. She'd barely dealt with her own issues of loss, mostly buried them, run from them or kicked a ball hard to send them far away.

"Just show him love and listen to him. He hasn't talked much about his feelings, and Scott is hurting as much as him. I want to get them into counseling, but I'm giving them time to get used to each other, and hopefully, for Scott to come to me on his own."

"But why did Scott need to quit the league to take over his brother's job? Surely, there's someone else."

"It's more than that. Hank and Kristen named Scott as Henry's guardian."

"What about his grandparents?"

"It's what Kristen and Hank wanted for Henry. Scott's parents aren't in the best of health and are busy managing the hardware store, and Kristen's parents live in Atlanta. They wanted Henry raised in Woodley. Kristen loved this town, and the way everyone supports each other. They wanted Henry to have a dad who could throw a ball with him. I'm sure they didn't expect this all to happen, but it's how they wrote their will."

"I feel terrible. I am so selfish." Rainey slumped. "Scott must hate me."

"I doubt that, and you aren't selfish. You didn't know any of this."

"I practically threw my professional career in his face and then I turned Henry into a soccer fanatic. He might not hate me, but I doubt he wants to partner with me."

"Scott wants what's best for Henry, and Henry needs to work through his grief. If soccer helps him, I'm pretty sure Scott won't care what kind of ball is involved. Besides, this will give them something that can be all their own. They won't have anything from the past overshadowing their time together, and from what I've seen, they have a long way to go in their relationship."

"I can't imagine going from a professional athlete to a parent overnight. I wouldn't know where to begin. Scott must feel so lost, and to have all this happen just as he was moving up in the organization. All his dreams…gone." She snapped her fingers, but the words left a sour taste in her mouth. Was her soccer career really that important? Here was a child who no longer had a mother or a father. Regret knotted her insides. "I know that sounded selfish, but it all seems so unfair."

"This broken world is often unfair, but we must trust that God will work good even from the most devastating of circumstances." Grandpa straightened. "The longer I live, the more I see how God adjusts our perspectives, and if we trust Him and go to Him for discernment, He will direct our purposes and the results will undoubtedly be different than we planned, but it's been my experience they are often much better."

"I hope you're right." Rainey wanted to believe her grandpa, wanted to trust that God could work for good in this situation, but how? It all seemed so bleak and a little too familiar. She stood. "Are there some plastic cones around here?"

"In the storage shed." Grandpa pointed to the small structure at the end of the building. "What are you planning?"

"I'm not sure how to help a five-year-old deal with grief, but I do know how to run a soccer practice, so that's what I'll do." She jogged to the shed before any tears escaped. While her dad hadn't died, he'd left. Even if he'd returned eventually, it didn't make her pain any less real. Her mom had never been the same, had become a shell of the mother she'd once been, and now, she was basically gone, too. The truth was Rainey knew exactly how it felt to lose a parent, and she'd do anything to help Henry heal.

Chapter Two

The words on the requirements for a teacher's certificate blurred. Groaning, Scott dropped his head on the heap of paperwork stacked on his desk. How was he supposed to take care of Henry, coach a team to State, teach six periods of PE and complete this program for his teacher's certificate? All with less than five hours of sleep. At least he'd taken the right classes in college for the school district to get him a provisional certificate. He shoved the papers to the side. He had a couple of years to figure this all out.

For now, he needed to determine how to teach the square-dance unit. He rubbed his forehead as the dancers moved across his computer screen in silence, since he'd muted the caller. Rainey wasn't alone in her opinion of square dancing, but the principal insisted that every student learn the basics and participate in the annual Spring Festival. He'd learned from the music teacher that the principal participated in a monthly square-dance club and refused to see the style of dance die.

What he wouldn't give to return to living in a crowded apartment and eating ramen noodles. His only care had been how far he hit a baseball. Scott dropped his chin to his chest and massaged his temples. He needed more coffee. He'd woken too early, dreaming—or rather escaping a nightmare—that he was coaching soccer with Rainey Allen, but then he remembered it was his new reality.

Envy played a game of tug-of-war with guilt inside him. She was living his dream and could help him with Henry. Help he desperately needed. It was all too much. No wonder it crept into his subconscious. He'd been praying for a solution to his issues with Henry. He hadn't expected the answer to come in the form of his first crush, but he was no longer a middle-school boy. He could control his feelings and certainly his impulses. Besides, they weren't even friends. The way she'd challenged him felt more like a pitcher intent on striking him out, but winning wasn't fun if it was easy.

The door swooshed open, and he peered up.

"I'm so sorry, Scott." With concern etched above her slate-blue eyes, Rainey frowned as she stopped in front of his desk. So much for a formidable opponent. It'd been fun while it lasted.

"So they told you my sad story." He dropped his hands to the heavy wooden desk with a thud.

"I made y'all granola bars."

"You made granola bars?"

Rainey placed a plastic container in front of him. "Yes. Don't tell me you don't like granola bars. I can make muffins or something else."

"It's not that. In the six months that I've been here with Henry, we've never received granola bars. Casseroles by the dozens, pies, cakes, cookies and every kind of bread you can imagine." He peeled off the lid. Sure enough, granola bars cut in precise rectangles filled the box. "I didn't know homemade granola bars were even a thing." He lifted one and examined it. "This looks very healthy."

"I'm kind of into eating healthy with the whole professional-athlete thing. Aren't you?"

"Baseball players aren't really known for being exceptionally healthy eaters, especially on the peanuts you're paid in the minor leagues." He broke the bar in half. What was in this thing? It appeared to be chocolate chips, but he'd been fooled before with raisins. He sniffed. "Smells like peanut butter."

"They're peanut-butter chocolate-chip. Oh, I hope y'all aren't allergic to peanuts." She cringed. "I should've asked. I can make them with something different. Grandma had peanut butter and chocolate chips at the house, so I used those, but I can do them without nuts."

"We don't have any nut allergies, but we may be allergic to green foods." He took a bite of the bar. The chocolate and peanut butter coated his tongue in a perfect mixture of salty and sweet. These were definitely better than another chicken casserole. Maybe even Henry would eat them. He had to start eating something besides sugary cereal. "I'd be happy to sample any variety you want to try. These are delicious." He shoved the rest of the bar in his mouth and reached for another.

Rainey's shoulders relaxed as a smile brightened her face. "I'm glad you like them but save some for Henry."

"You mean you didn't make him his own box?"

"Ha ha. But in all seriousness, what you're doing for him, what you've given up, what you've been through, you deserve a lot more than granola bars. Henry is blessed to have you as his guardian." She twisted the end of her blond ponytail. "I hope we can call a truce and leave our past in the past. We were stupid kids the last time I was here, and if we'll be working together, I think it would be better to be friends than enemies."

"Rainey, I never wanted to be your enemy." If anything, he'd wanted to be her dance partner, but like most adolescent boys, he'd chosen teasing her to show his affection instead of kindness. *Fool*. To this day, she was the only girl or woman who'd caused actual tingles to scramble up his arms.

"Well—" she glanced down "—I guess I remember things differently."

"No, I probably acted like the moronic kid I was, but I'm happy to forgive and forget if you are."

"Of course." She released her hair and met his gaze. "All is forgiven and forgotten."

"And one last thing." Because this conversation was getting way too harmonious, and he liked the fiery Rainey. "You have to promise to refrain from throwing me into walls and breaking my arm."

"Again, I'm sorry. I promise I didn't mean to." She rubbed her forehead. "I seriously don't want to cause you any more grief, and I want to help Henry any way I can. What do you say?" She caught her lower lip between her teeth.

While her vulnerability warmed him, he couldn't work with someone who was always shielding him from the truth. She was competitive and confident, and while he thought this version of Rainey was sweet, he liked the one who held her own and told him off when he needed it.

"For the record, I was joking about you throwing me into any walls. I think I might have a little more size on you now." Scott straightened his spine, thrusting out his chest.

Surely, that would get more of a response out of her, but she merely nodded, maintaining a pleasant expression.

"Rainey, seriously, I don't need another person treating me like I might break down at the slightest objection. Yesterday was the first time someone told me 'no' since I moved home." He snapped the lid on the box. "It was nice, almost normal."

"Um, okay. I guess." She shrugged. "But—"

"No *buts*." He came around the desk, extending his hand. "Do we have a deal?"

"Just to be clear." She grasped his hand. "I'm not supposed to hold back. You want the truth even if it hurts." She tightened her grip and stared back at him.

"Even if it hurts." Holding her focus, he matched her strength as energy surged up his arm with those irritatingly wonderful tingles. Who would relent first? Not him; he certainly didn't mind the warmth flooding him as he held her hand. He dove into those deep blue eyes and reveled in this moment of connection, of being alive. He'd been so shut off, so careful to hem in his emotions, but something about Rainey gave him the freedom to let his pulse rage.

"Deal." The word escaped her lips on a breath as she jerked free. Retreating from him, she adjusted the colorful band around her head as a blush tinged her cheeks. "I need to get to my workout." She fled to the free weights.

"Okay." He sat, placing his elbows on the desk and bowing over the paperwork. Had she felt the connection between them? Something had certainly taken the breath from her. But he needed to remember everything with Rainey was temporary. He'd already watched Dawn split when faced with moving to this small town. They'd dated on and off for two years, but she'd sprinted away like she was stealing home.

Rainey would help him get over this hurdle with Henry, and then she'd be gone before things got complicated. It was the only way this would work.

After lunch the next day, Rainey hauled her bag of balls out to the field. The afternoon sun blazed high in the clear blue sky, taking the chill out of the January day. Scott was supposed to meet her during his free period for his first lesson. After that awkward moment when they'd shaken hands, she'd spent the next hour avoiding him and exhausting her jittery nerves with an intense weight workout. They may have put their past behind them, but his touch set her nerves on high alert.

It was probably just muscle memory. The last time they'd held hands was in that terrible square-dance class. When she'd realized she was the target for him to win the kissing dare, she'd had no choice but to dodge him. A familiar surge of adrenaline pumped through her. She hadn't meant to hurt him, but he'd hurt her, too.

Although Scott seemed different, and his apology seemed sincere. Still, it was hard for her to know. She never got people right, especially men. It didn't really matter. While partnering with Scott hadn't been in her plans, it would keep her busy, which would leave less time to worry. And since he was on board, she could train like she needed to. Besides, she had to do this for Henry. That kid deserved something to go right in his world.

In the corner of the outfield, Rainey dropped the bag near the portable goal her grandpa had helped her set up. Scott would be happy that it wouldn't interfere with practices, and they could move it if there was a game. She needed to check the high-school baseball schedule for the first game.

Concentrating on her hamstrings, Rainey began her warmup. She stood with her feet slightly wider than her hips and reached for her left ankle. The sharp pain persisted until her muscles relaxed. When she played, she put it out of her mind after a proper warmup and stretch. Hopefully, by March, her dad could arrange a tryout with one of the National Women's Soccer League teams. If not, she'd probably head back to Europe or Australia.

She switched to her right ankle and closed her eyes, taking long controlled breaths, as her trainer had instructed. The straining muscle needed oxygen. Inhaling deeply, the smell of the grass drew her attention to the future, to the goals she'd set so long ago. If she trained hard enough, she would get a contract. It would happen. This was her time. She was ready.

"Hey there. I sure hope you don't expect me to touch my toes," Scott said, interrupting her.

Rainey opened her eyes, and two orange clay-stained cleats appeared in her line of sight. She pressed her palms to her thighs as she slowly rolled her body to standing.

Scott sported a pair of crimson athletic shorts over his massive quads. *Impressive.* She'd expected him to be in good shape given his broad shoulders and the way the sleeves of his golf shirt hugged his biceps, but the definition of his leg muscles had been hidden in his loose-fitting khaki pants. Realizing she was staring at him, she jerked her focus to his face. *Get it together, Rainey.* He's just another athlete.

Heat skittered up her neck, and she lowered the zipper on her jacket. "Just don't come crying to me when you can't walk tomorrow." She pointed at his dirty shoes. "What are those?"

"Cleats. Figured they'd work as well for soccer as baseball."

"You can't play soccer with metal spikes."

"I'm not playing soccer. Just coaching."

"Fine, but we'll need to get Henry some soccer cleats." She tightened her ponytail. "If you're not stretching, we can begin with the basic warmup drills that we'll teach the kids. You ready?"

"Born ready." Scott cocked his head.

"We'll see." Rainey ignored him, sticking to the task at hand. "Let's jog to the fence. Once we get there, we'll jog backward to this spot. Let's do five sets."

"Got it." Scott jogged beside Rainey at a comfortable pace. "This isn't so bad."

"With the kids, I want to teach them the best dynamic exercises. They must warm up using the types of movements they'll use in a game." They reached the fence and started back.

"Believe it or not, we warm up in baseball, too."

"I'm sure you do. Right before you stand around, guarding your base."

"We run, too."

"Right. For what, a max of ten, fifteen seconds?"

"Better be faster than that if you don't want to get tagged out." He paused at the bag of balls. "Race you to the fence."

"Sure." She grinned. "Go." She leapt into a sprint, beating him off the start, but Scott zipped by her side in milliseconds. "You win this time." Rainey slapped the chain links. "But how are you going backward?" She pumped her arms and took short, quick strides down her line.

"I guess this is when you tell me that soccer requires more stamina and technique, so it's a harder sport."

"If you say so."

"I didn't." He picked up his pace. "One day, I'll put you through one of my practices. Have you ever swung a bat?"

"Never had time." Returning to their starting spot, Rainey stopped. "I trained a minimum of five days a week on the field and at least three days a week in the weight room plus games on weekends. There wasn't time for other sports." She took a sip from her water bottle. "How about you? Did you play other sports?"

"Some football until I got hit so hard that I saw stars. I wasn't much of a basketball player, and we didn't have many other sports."

"I remember that from my year of middle school."

"When did you get into soccer?"

"I played rec ball when I was young, five and six." With her toe, she rolled a ball out of the bag. "My dad was my coach, but once he started law school, he didn't have time, and my mom put me in ballet classes. As you might recall, I wasn't much of a dancer." She shot the ball into the upper right corner of the goal.

"You seem graceful when you kick like that." He tossed a ball between his large hands. "I wouldn't judge your dance skills on your brief encounter with the square dance. You should probably blame your partner."

"Maybe." She smiled, her heart warming. "Anyway, the next exercise is to shuffle sideways, like this."

"Got it." He shuffled along with her. "When did you get back into soccer?"

"After my parents' divorce." She paused and slid in the opposite direction. "Over the summer, I visited my dad in Jacksonville, and he put me in soccer camps. I was pretty good, and they invited me to play on one of the club teams. My dad was totally into it, so he signed the contract, and as they say, the rest is history."

"It's kind of surprising that we still don't have a high-school soccer team, but it hasn't caught on. Besides catching a few World Cup games, I have no idea about the sport. I'll need complete written instructions."

"Already on it." Rainey reached into her backpack and pulled out the binder she'd prepared for him. "This covers everything we're doing and the rules of the game, plus the positions on the field."

"You think of everything."

"I may be a bit of a perfectionist, especially when it comes to soccer. It would drive me nuts to watch you do everything wrong."

Scott chuckled. "I hope I don't disappoint you, Coach."

"I'm managing my expectations."

"Wow. Thanks for the vote of confidence."

"Kidding." She took the binder. "We still have work to do. High-knees are next."

"When do we get to kick the balls?"

Rainey drew her knees up to her palms in quick succession. "Didn't anyone ever tell you patience is a virtue?"

"Just want to make sure I know how to coach this team before you leave."

"Don't worry. You'll be ready. I'll make sure." And maybe working with him would be fun. This session made her optimistic. Maybe they really could be friends. It was nice to have someone to talk to who understood her and what she was going through without a lot of explanation. For most of her life, she'd felt alone, but training with Scott felt oddly comfortable.

After another late night playing *FIFA World Cup* with Henry, Scott trudged into his nephew's bedroom as the first rays of sunlight filtered through the limbs of the magnolia tree outside his window. Scott had express-shipped the video game to surprise Henry, and if his uncle's new soccer knowledge impressed a certain soccer player with a blond ponytail, all the better. They'd played the game every night since it'd arrived. Unfortunately, while Scott was learning a lot about soccer, his relationship with Henry was still far from ideal.

Scott scanned the baseball-themed bedroom. His mom said Kristen and Hank had surprised Henry with the new big-boy room for his fifth birthday. Would they need to redecorate with a soccer theme for his sixth? A family picture taken last Easter was perched on the table between Henry's bed and the wall. Poor kid. His world could never be the same.

Henry's arm was slung over Champ, and Champ's paw rested on Henry's back. The yellow Lab took his job as Henry's protector so seriously that Scott's job as guardian seemed almost unnecessary. Scott had given Champ to Hank and Kristen as a wedding present, and they'd treated the puppy like their firstborn child. When Henry joined their family, Champ took on the role of big brother. Scott ruffled the dog's hair. "Time to get up, sleepyheads."

Both boy and dog groaned.

"Come on, Henry." Scott folded back the boy's quilt. "Remember, we're going shopping with Rainey for soccer cleats." He still couldn't believe she'd agreed to spend the morning with them, but maybe she was learning not to hate him. Besides being grateful for everything she was doing to help Henry, Scott was enjoying their time together, maybe a little too much.

Henry rolled onto his back and stretched his arms above his head, rousing Champ from his slumber. "Time to get up, boy."

"What do you want for breakfast?" Scott asked.

"I'm not hungry."

"You need to eat something." Henry couldn't continue like this. *They* couldn't continue like this. Scott's best efforts to meet Henry's needs kept failing. Before the accident, they'd always had fun when Scott visited, playing Henry's favorite video games, throwing the baseball and even stuffing their faces at holiday dinners. But as much as Scott tried to re-create those situations, Henry showed little interest in forming a relationship. Scott's mom kept telling him to be patient, but he was used to winning, whether at games or with people. He didn't know how to fail. And he was determined to be a great father figure for Henry.

Champ hopped from the bed and nudged Henry. At least Champ wouldn't starve under Scott's watch.

Henry dropped his legs over the side of the twin bed. "Do we have any more of Rainey's granola bars?" Soccer and

Rainey were the first things Henry had cared about since the accident.

Thankfully, he'd barely acknowledged Dawn's presence during their time together, and to her credit, she'd tried to comfort him. Scott's stomach knotted. What would happen when Rainey left? He could learn the game, but the last thing Henry needed was someone else he loved leaving him.

"Uncle Scott, do we have any of Rainey's granola bars?" Henry whined, tugging on the edge of Scott's flannel shirt.

"Buddy, we finished them last night." Scott shifted his focus to Henry's brown eyes—just like Hank's, just like his—but the brightness was gone. Scott's heart crumbled along with his willpower. Rainey would leave, but until then, she was the bridge that he needed to meet Henry, and hopefully, they'd have moved far beyond it and this ravine by the time she left.

Scott hugged Henry to his side. "How about we get donuts on the way to the sports store?"

"Okay. Come on, Champ." The twosome ambled down the hall, and Henry let the dog out the back door. They had this routine mastered. After Champ finished his business, Henry would follow the dog to the kitchen and watch him eat.

With a sigh, Scott left them and hustled into the living room. It looked like a tornado had blown through with clothes, dirty dishes and dust. He'd meant to straighten up before they'd gone to bed but it'd been late. He checked his watch. Rainey would be here in less than ten minutes. "Henry, I need you to grab all your clothes and put them in the laundry basket." Scott circled the coffee table, collecting dishes. "Henry, please hurry."

"Coming." But Henry merely strolled by with Champ.

"Dude, Champ knows his way. I need your help."

"Just a minute." Henry continued to follow Champ.

"No, Henry—now." Scott winced. He sounded like his dad, but Henry returned and collected his clothes. This wasn't the relationship Scott wanted. He wanted Henry to feel loved. They needed to be friends. "Thanks for helping. You can get two donuts, any flavor." Scott darted to the kitchen and loaded the dishes into the dishwasher.

After he started it, he turned to survey the scene. Henry sat on the floor petting Champ. It would take more effort to get him to help than do it himself. Thankfully, the house was small, and with school and practice, they weren't home long enough to make too much of a mess.

Scott zipped around the kitchen, wiping the counters and table. "Henry, please put on some jeans and a sweatshirt. It's cold outside."

"Yes, sir." As the boy made his way to his room, a knock sounded at the door.

"Please hurry. Rainey's here," Scott called as he approached the door.

"Yeah." Henry trotted down the hall.

Scott opened the door. "Good morning."

"Good morning. I brought muffins." Rainey smiled brightly above a plastic container, her normally slate eyes almost blue in the morning light.

"Come in." Scott's stomach flipped as he nearly stumbled backward. She was the best kind of beautiful woman—unpretentious and unaware of her natural beauty. Her face was free of makeup except for a soft glisten of what he assumed was gloss on her lips. She wore her blond hair in her standard ponytail, and the youthfulness of her appearance seemed unburdened even though worry often etched her forehead while she trained.

"Hey, Coach Rainey!" Henry ran between them fully dressed and bounced like he'd downed a dozen energy drinks.

"What a welcome." Rainey gave the box to Henry. "I got up early this morning and baked these muffins for you."

"Yummy." He snatched out a muffin and stuffed it into his mouth.

Closing the door, Scott caught the most delightful scent of citrus lingering in the air that tempted him to move closer to Rainey. "What's in those muffins?"

"They're actually really healthy."

"Forgive me if I don't believe you and need to taste for myself." He lifted a muffin, smelled it, pinched off a morsel and examined it. "Are those c-a-r-r-o-t-s?"

Rainey nodded. "I promise there's so many vitamins packed in those you can skip your veggies the rest of the day."

"Shh." He glanced at Henry, but the boy was chomping on his second muffin, so Scott popped a bite into his mouth. Cinnamon and sugar and some tantalizing spice skipped across his tongue. "Delicious. You sure you want to play soccer? You could be a very successful baker."

"Why do you think I learned to make all this stuff? I needed to be healthy, and on my salary, I couldn't afford the right kinds of food. I've become somewhat of a team chef, and I love it."

"These are the best, Coach." Henry reached for another muffin.

"That's probably enough, buddy. We don't want you to get sick." Rainey lifted the box.

"Here, I'll take that to the kitchen," Scott said.

"How many will you steal before you return?"

"None. I'm saving them all for Henry." He probably should explain that Henry refused to eat anything but cereal, but it made him feel like such a failure.

"Really?" As she studied him, the corners of her lips tipped up with admiration. "You're a pretty great guy." She gave the box to him, holding his gaze. "And you're constantly surprising me." She spun to face Henry.

"I hope that's a good thing."

"I think so. Henry—" she clapped "—ready to go find you some soccer cleats?"

"I want some just like yours."

Of course, he did. If Rainey wasn't so great, Scott might be jealous.

Chapter Three

On Tuesday, three children arrived with Henry for the first soccer clinic, and while they hadn't made a lot of progress learning soccer, they'd laughed a lot, mostly at Scott's expense. Normally, when Rainey's plans went awry, she simmered with frustration, but to her surprise, she didn't mind. She loved teaching Henry and the other kids. Of course, her perfectionist tendencies stood no chance against Scott's doomed dribble demonstration. From the moment he tripped and somersaulted over the ball, she'd adjusted her expectations and let joy fill her. It was fun to laugh and play without the stress of her career hanging over every touch.

With Rainey's changed perspective, she greeted Scott and the children Thursday afternoon. "Who thinks they can dribble better than Coach Scott?"

"Me!" The kids all shot up their hands, snickering.

"I believe balls are to be thrown, not kicked." Scott slung a ball at Rainey.

But she bounced it off her chest and proceeded to juggle it between her knees. "We'll have a throwing lesson at another session. Throwing can be very important to soccer." She popped the ball to Scott.

"So, kids, what's the first thing we need to do?" Rainey asked.

"Stretch and warm up," Mindy answered.

"Correct, so let's jog around the field two times." Rainey led the kids, keeping a slow pace. "Y'all are going to be so fast."

"I'm the fastest." Liam ran ahead.

Emma chased after him. "No, you're not."

"Whoa." Scott caught up to them. "This isn't a race."

"Yeah." Mindy pointed her finger at the others. "We're only warming up our muscles, remember."

"But, I think—"

Scott dropped a hand on Liam's shoulder. "Nope. We do what Coach Rainey says if we want to be the best soccer players."

"Yes, sir." Liam sneered at Mindy as she skipped by him.

Once they'd completed their jog, Rainey directed the kids through a modified version of her stretch routine. At the first training, she learned that the positions that had become natural to her weren't as easy for the children, or apparently, Scott, who'd groaned and then toppled over, causing a round of giggles from all the kids except Mindy. She'd glared at him and offered to be the assistant coach, even though she was the same age as the rest of the children. Scott's comic relief helped Rainey loosen up and relate better to the children.

Today, Scott refrained from too much silliness as they went through the stretches and then they all lined up with their balls.

Rainey lifted her foot. "What part of my foot should I not use?"

"Your toe," Henry said.

"Correct. We want to use the sides of our foot to move the ball." Rainey tapped her ball with the edge of both sides of her foot. "Everyone give it a try with each foot ten times."

Liam pouted. "When do we get to kick the ball in the goal?"

"If everyone focuses and plays nice, I'll let y'all shoot for the last ten minutes."

"Yay!" The kids and Scott cheered, filling Rainey with an unexpected surge of thrills. This playful side of him didn't annoy her at all. Nope. His silliness disarmed her, freeing her to show her true self.

At the end of practice, Rainey, Scott and Henry stored the equipment. But in the parking lot, a man paced, a grimace fixing his features taut. He turned out to be the father of the varsity team's first baseman. One glance at the unhappy, possibly angry, man, and Rainey volunteered to walk Henry home.

"Yes!" Henry pulled his fists into his side. "Will you please make supper and dessert, too?"

"Sure, buddy."

"Just fix him a bowl of cereal with marshmallows and shapes." Scott backed away. "The key's under the bulldog by the back door."

But Rainey couldn't feed anyone something so unhealthy, so she texted her grandma a list of things to bring over. Thankfully, she'd already stocked up on healthy ingredients at the grocery store because she loved creating nutritious dishes.

As they strolled, Henry's small hand wrapped around Rainey's, sending waves of warmth through her. She'd never experienced this kind of unconditional adoration. Although Henry did want her to make him supper and dessert, so maybe he was manipulating her, but it didn't feel like that.

Henry swung their arms. "What are you making?"

"Something yummy. What's your favorite food?"

"I dunno." Henry's swinging slowed.

"What about mac and cheese?"

"I guess." His hand went limp. Maybe she should give in to the cereal request. It probably wouldn't hurt him.

"Henry, is cereal your favorite food?"

"I dunno. I'm not hungry."

"But you said you wanted me to make you supper and dessert." Rainey squatted in front of him.

Henry diverted his gaze to his shoes. "I'm sorry."

"It's okay, buddy." Rainey squeezed his hand. "But my grandma is bringing all the food, and I think you'll like what I planned. You liked my granola bars and muffins, didn't you?"

He nodded, but his grip remained weak.

"Tell you what—you can help me, and then you can decide if you want to eat what we make. It'll be fun."

"Okay."

"Great." Rainey stood. "You can be my sous chef." She swung his arm gently as they strolled to the back door. "Do you know what that means?"

"No."

"It's a fancy French word for the person who is the chef's top helper." Beside the door, she flipped over the small concrete bulldog statue and retrieved the house key. "But first you need to wash your hands." She unlocked the kitchen door.

"Hi, boy." Henry kneeled on the threshold, a yellow Lab licking his cheek. "This is Champ. He needs to go out and play."

"Okay." Rainey held the door for the joyful dog. "Wash really well."

"Yes, ma'am." Henry slung off his bag before climbing on a stool in front of the sink and turning on the water.

"Good job, buddy." Rainey crouched to put the key in its place.

"Yoo-hoo." Grandma rounded the corner with two large grocery bags. "I got everything you asked for. That colorful pasta made of vegetables was a great idea. I sure hope Henry will give it a try."

"Once we put it in my two-cheese mac and cheese, he won't know the difference." Rainey took the bags. "Thanks. Can you stick around for a minute?"

"Sure."

"Just let me put this in the kitchen." Rainey placed the bags on the table.

Henry showed his palms. "All clean."

"Great job." She passed him a dish towel. "I need to talk to my grandma and then we'll get started. Can you do me a big favor and put the food from the bags on the counter?"

"Yes, ma'am." Henry hopped off the stool.

Rainey slipped outside and closed the door behind her. "What's going on with Henry's eating?"

"Not much." Grandma frowned. "He barely eats at school. His grandma Judy asked me to pray for him and Scott. From what I understand, he only eats cereal, but more than that, he and Scott aren't bonding. She's really concerned. Scott won't ask for much help, and he seems completely defeated. Henry is seeing the school counselor, but he seems so lost. Poor, precious child. We're all praying for them, but healing takes time." She took Rainey's hand. "Honey, Henry seems to be really taken with you and soccer."

"I don't know how to help him."

"Just keep doing what you're doing. Love him and listen to him. Hopefully, he'll open up." She smiled. "And, honey, Scott seems to be pretty taken with you as well."

"What are you talking about? He's just my assistant coach. We barely know each other." Besides, dating was the last thing on her mind. As warmth skittered up her neck, Rainey slipped free of her grandma's hold. This conversation needed to end. She only wanted to help Henry. Scott would never be interested in her in that way. Guys didn't see her like that— never had. She reached for the doorknob. "My focus is my soccer career, and with the exception of my coaches, men have never been a part of it."

"Okay, okay. Don't get your apron in a tangle. I just thought I saw some sparks." She waved her hand dismissively. "Now, honey, I know you like to find the best way to do things, but Scott needs your friendship more than your direction. Be gentle with him if you want to give him advice."

"Honestly, I can't imagine I'd have any advice on how to parent a little boy who lost both his parents." Her stomach knotted as a stream of sweat formed on her spine. This was all too much. What had her grandma seen between her and Scott? They'd just been training with kids. This is why she didn't complicate her life with dating, not that she'd received a lot of offers. She always read people wrong, and a person would get upset, and she rarely understood why.

"No parents are given a manual. You're more intuitive than you give yourself credit for. From what I hear, you've already gotten Henry to eat more than he has in months."

"I guess, but it's just food. Anything else is a job for some-one else."

"God put you here for a reason, and I don't think it was only to avoid your dad."

"I'm not avoiding him. I wanted to spend time with y'all." She tried to turn the knob, but her palms slipped.

"No matter the reason." Grandma shooed her hand as she backed down the drive. "You're here, and Henry and Scott need you. See you later."

"God, if You plan to use me, You better help a lot. I sure can't do this on my own." Rainey dried her palms on her leggings as Champ nuzzled her knee. Interesting answer to prayer, but she'd take it.

As Scott entered the kitchen, the aroma of garlic and cheese greeted him. He could get used to coming home to a delicious supper and a beautiful woman. Too bad Rainey wasn't interested in the position, but it wouldn't hurt to drop a subtle hint.

"Honey, I'm home." Or not so subtle. He chuckled, dropping his backpack on the floor by Henry's.

"Very funny. We're in the living room," Rainey called. "And we may have saved you some of Henry's soon-to-be-world-famous very cheesy mac."

"Can't wait." Scott rushed from the kitchen and the swarm of butterflies attacking his insides. As he entered the room, he stopped short. Rainey and Henry beamed at him from their spots on a plaid blanket. His breath quivered at the back of his throat, and he dropped his chin before they saw the tears threatening to escape.

"We made a picnic inside," Henry said. "Champ tried to join us, so we put him out."

"I hope this is okay. Henry said y'all eat in here most of the time."

"It's great. I can't wait to dig in." He swiped under his eyes as nonchalantly as possible, while he rounded the couch and took a spot on the corner of the blanket. "What happened to a bowl of cereal?"

"You're welcome to make yourself whatever you want, but I'm pretty sure you knew this would be the result of your suggestion." She smirked.

"Not quite this." He gestured to the display. "But thank you. It was really nice of you, and I can't wait to taste this cheesy mac." He ruffled Henry's hair to keep his hand from grasping Rainey's. As attracted as he might have been to Rainey before this moment, the gratitude he felt for her helping Henry doubled his interest in exploring something more with her.

Henry ducked away from Scott. "Rainey let me help, and we made dessert, too."

"But it's a surprise." Placing her finger to her lips, Rainey exchanged a look with Henry.

"Guess I better hurry and eat my mac and cheese." He scooped a large bite into his mouth. The cheese and noodles melted together with a perfect blend of subtle flavors. Even the garlic that smelled so strong was tamed in the dish. "Delicious."

"Glad you like it. I hope everything is okay with your player."

"He's fine. His dad's just worried about how his son's grades will affect scholarship chances."

"I'm glad it was nothing too serious." On her knees, Rainey stacked the bowls. "I'll take our dishes to the sink while you finish. Henry, you want to help me get dessert?"

"Yes." Henry sprinted to the kitchen.

"Rainey, thanks again for this…all of it." He met her gaze. "I can't believe how excited Henry is about eating, but I am surprised there are no vegetables."

"You just don't see them." She grinned. "And you're welcome, but I'd like to talk to you about Henry. I discovered something tonight."

"Okay. Can you stay until he goes to bed?"

"Sure."

"Rainey, hurry up!" Henry shouted.

"Yes, sir." Rainey hopped to her feet.

"Dude, be patient. She's coming." Scott finished off his bowl of cheesy mac, listening to their whispers.

"Are you ready?" Henry peeked into the room.

"I can hardly wait." Scott gave him a thumbs-up.

"Close your eyes."

After Scott closed his eyes, their footsteps drew closer until he heard Henry's excited breathing.

"Open." Henry held a plate in front of him with what appeared to be chocolate peanut-butter cups. "Wait 'til you see what we hid in the middle."

Scott took one of the cold treats and bit it in half. He savored the combo of salty peanut butter and dark chocolate and something else sweet. He studied the morsel that was left. "Banana?"

"Yes." Henry took one for himself.

Rainey held up two fingers. "Only two, Henry."

"But it's so yummy and healfee," Henry said while he chewed.

"He has you there."

Rainey ignored Scott as she directed a pointed look at Henry. "If you eat them all tonight, not only will you have a bellyache, but you also won't have any for tomorrow."

"Okay." Henry chose his second, nibbling it in small bites.

"I think Henry's going to need some more cooking lessons." Scott popped another treat in his mouth.

"Yes." Henry nodded like a bobblehead doll.

"I'm glad y'all like it, but maybe you ought to join us for our next lesson." She tucked her bottom lip between her teeth. Her request had seemed innocent enough, so why was she avoiding his gaze?

Rainey was different than the women he'd dated in the past. They were forward and experienced women who knew how to charm a man with precision. Until this moment, she'd treated him like a buddy or a competitor, but never like she was concerned about her words or actions. It was one of the things that he liked about her. She was straightforward, no silly games. Maybe he was reading too much into her actions. It could mean anything.

"I'd be happyto," Scott said flatly, being sure he didn't insert anything romantic.

"Great." Rainey rose. "I can do the dishes and clean the kitchen while you get Henry bathed and ready for bed. Sorry, we only got his hands cleaned before we started dinner."

"Aren't we playing *FIFA World Cup* tonight?" Henry crossed his arms. "I'm not tired."

"Maybe we take tonight off. It's getting late." Scott stood.

"But I want to show Rainey."

"We'll do it another night, buddy," Rainey said. "I need to get to bed early because I go for a long run first thing in the morning. It's part of my training. Okay?"

When Henry didn't respond, Scott lifted the boy to his feet. "Let's go, Henry."

"I don't want to."

"Please, buddy. You need to get a good night's sleep, so you can be a great soccer player like Rainey."

"I'm not tired. Please, just one game."

"We'll see." Scott clasped Henry's shoulder and directed him toward the bathroom. "Maybe if you take a quick bath and get your pj's on really fast."

"Fine." Henry stomped out of the room. "I'm getting Champ first."

"Thanks for trying." Scott glanced at Rainey as he followed Henry. Her forehead wrinkled, but she spared him a small smile. She wasn't judging him, but it still felt like another fail.

He shouldn't have negotiated with Henry, but he couldn't have him go into a total meltdown in front of Rainey. Besides, the kid had lost his parents. Surely, one round of a video game wouldn't ruin him. As the tension crept in, Scott massaged his neck. Why was everything with Henry two steps forward and ten steps back?

After wrestling Henry through bath time, Scott slumped on the couch and handed over the video-game controller to Henry. "Just ten minutes and then straight to bed." The heaviness of failure settled inside him as he tried not to think about Rainey's opinion, but what did she know about raising kids? Then again, she'd gotten Henry to eat something besides cereal.

Henry bounced on the couch. "Do you want to play, Coach?"

"I prefer the real thing." Rainey lowered a piercing gaze on him, but Henry wasn't giving in this time.

Shifting his attention to Rainey, Scott shrugged. "If you need to go, we can talk tomorrow."

"That's okay. I can wait a few minutes." She settled on the other side of Henry, and Champ dropped his head in her lap. "Well, it's good to see you, too. Did you enjoy your pasta?" She scratched the dog's head. "I hope that's okay. Henry insisted on giving him some, and I didn't think plain pasta would hurt."

"It's fine." At least Rainey had also given in to the boy. Scott focused on his watch, counting his breaths as seconds. What would he do if Henry refused to cooperate? He almost always let the boy have his own way. He couldn't stand to watch him cry. All he wanted was for Henry to be happy.

After eight minutes, sweat collected under Scott's collar. The moment of truth was coming too soon and not fast enough. What would the verdict be? *Please, Lord.* It was a desperate thing to do, but he needed help. The last minute went by in no time, and Scott stood. "Alright, Henry. It's bedtime."

Henry snatched the controller to his chest. "The game isn't over."

"I'm sorry, but you can play more tomorrow. Right now, it's bedtime." Scott pried the remote from Henry's grasp.

Henry's lip trembled as he turned to face Rainey.

"Good night, Henry." She hugged him.

"Good night, Coach." Henry shot a look of disdain at Scott before shuffling to his room with Champ at his side.

"I'll just make sure he's tucked in." Scott hurried to Henry's room, and to his surprise, found the boy curled up with Champ.

"Good night, Henry. Love you." Scott closed the door and joined Rainey on the couch. "Sorry about all of that. You must think I'm such a softy."

"You're doing your best. You've both been through a lot." She twisted the end of her ponytail. "My grandma says I need to be careful about the way I give advice. Apparently, I can come across as critical." She dropped her hair. "And intimidating."

He chuckled. "I think I can handle it."

"Are you sure?"

"We agreed that you'd be honest with me, remember?"

She worried her lips, studying him.

"Seriously, Rainey, I apparently need some help, and trust me, it takes a lot for me to admit that. I'm more of a work-hard-and-you'll-achieve-your-goal kind of a guy, but this parenting thing doesn't come with a playbook." He grabbed at the base of his head, hating the tension that attacked him. This wasn't him. He was fun, a winner. Some even referred to him as a hometown hero. Although he hardly thought playing professional baseball was anything heroic, but he certainly had never been called a loser.

"Henry needs you to be firm. I'm guessing y'all were more like buddies when you were just his fun uncle. Then you could buy him ice cream and donuts and let him stay up late with you playing video games." She gestured in the direction of the television as if it was a crate of processed food.

"I thought he needed time to heal and get used to me."

"You might be right, but he doesn't have any problem obeying me."

"I've noticed." He slapped the cushion between them.

"I know you're used to winning, and I'm sure you hate it as much as I do when people repeat that saying about it being how you play the game that matters, but this isn't a game, and it does matter how you play. For what it's worth, and I get that I'm not much of an authority, but I think you're doing your best." Rainey scooted closer and patted his hand. It was a friendly, comforting gesture. Still, her touch, not to mention her words of encouragement, sent tingles skipping up his arm straight to his heart like a ball racing over the grass of the outfield. The kind of hit that might not result in a home run but definitely got the batter on base. Who was this woman?

He wrenched his attention from their hands. "Thanks for that."

"Sure." She removed her fingers, enabling him to breathe easier. "And this eating thing with Henry." She retreated to her spot, too far away from him, but he needed to concentrate on Henry. Besides, she obviously wasn't having similar reactions to their close encounters.

"I'm aware that feeding him endless bowls of sugary cereal is not a long-term solution, but I was afraid he'd die of malnutrition."

"Actually, I think it has something to do with the dishes. You may have noticed we only used white bowls tonight."

"I was more focused on what was in the bowls."

"Well, Henry showed me those bowls. They were in the back of a closet in what I guess was your sister-in-law's craft room. Did she paint all the dishes in the kitchen?"

"And the dishes at my parents' house." He slapped his forehead. "That was her job. She sold them at my parents' store and online."

"I think he equates most parts of mealtime with a feeling of loss."

"He's refused to sit at the kitchen table and insisted on

using the same bowl for his cereal at every meal. I just didn't make the connection. I'm such a fool."

"No, you're not. You got a lot thrown at you. You're—"

He raised his hand. "Do not say I'm doing great, again."

She bit her lip.

"Sorry, I didn't mean to cut you off." He lowered his hand. "You may be trying to sound encouraging, but you've known the kid for what, a week, and already you know more about him than me."

"He struggled to overcome the food thing today, but he didn't want to upset me, and so he figured out a compromise."

"It helps that your food is way too delicious to pass up."

Laughing, she stood. "I better go. I have an early morning appointment with the rooster at the Lindsey farm."

"That's a long way to run. Glad my sport is short distance." Scott held the door. "Thanks again, Rainey. I'll mention all of this to Henry's counselor."

She stepped outside. "The leftovers are in the fridge, and a few ingredients that we can use when I come over next time."

Next time. His eyebrows bounced before he could stop them. "Looking forward to it."

She scrutinized him like she might find the answer for his odd behavior written on his forehead. "Great. See you later." She gave a quick wave and fled.

Cringing, he retreated into the house. At least she only thought he was odd and not crushing on her.

Chapter Four

With tires squealing, Scott shot the jeep into the last empty parking spot. Nothing had gone right this morning. He'd tried to be firm with Henry. The kid could not wear his ninja costume to church. His mom might be full of grace on most things when it came to Scott's parenting decisions, but she'd come right out of the choir loft and scold them both if Henry didn't look presentable. Not to mention, she'd feel compelled to revisit the cost of the costume with all the unnecessary accessories, but Scott hadn't even realized Henry needed a costume for the community Trunk-or-Treat last fall until a few days before the event.

Only a couple of months after he'd been thrust into his new role, Scott had ordered the costume Henry showed the most interest in, but they should've skipped the fall event. Henry had moped around the cars, collecting candy from people who tried to smile but couldn't hide their own grief. For Scott, the welcome expressions quickly morphed to startled recognition and then the remarks of how much he resembled his identical twin brother. He'd tried not to blow off their insensitive words, but they grated at his fragile ego. Obviously, everyone, including him, thought if one twin perished, it should not have been the one with a young son who needed a father and a town who needed a baseball coach.

Sure, everyone cheered on Scott's pro-ball career, but it was just baseball. There was no comparison. Hank was a great husband, father, coach, son and—especially—brother.

Loss emptied Scott, leaving a space for the brother who knew him best. But he didn't have time to wallow. He patted his brother's cross that hung around his neck, close to his heart.

"Let's go, Henry." Scott snatched his key from the ignition.

"I hate this shirt." Still strapped into his booster seat, Henry yanked at the collar of his button-down shirt.

"Sorry, dude." Scott lifted Henry to the ground and hustled them to the church. "We don't have time for this." As Scott opened the heavy wooden door, organ music greeted them, so they must not be too late.

In the sanctuary, Scott surveyed the nearby pews for an empty spot, avoiding the choir loft and his mom's scowl. Unfortunately, the back rows had filled up first.

"Good morning, guys. I saved y'all some seats." His dad appeared in his usher's uniform, navy suit with a striped tie. Must be the second Sunday of the month. Dad took Henry's hand and headed down the center aisle, while Scott followed closely behind.

After passing several available spots, Dad deposited them in the front row, and the organ music came to an abrupt stop, like Mrs. Cottrill was waiting until they took their seats. Scott cringed—the late arrivals' music. Mom would be furious, but at least they'd made it. When Champ had taken off after his arch-nemesis squirrel, Scott had almost given up.

But Scott wasn't a quitter, and he'd won the chase. He exhaled, dropping his chin to his chest.

"Long morning?" An elbow nudged his side, and he shot his gaze to the woman seated beside him—Rainey.

In his effort to avoid eye contact with the entire congregation, he'd missed her, and as he caught a whiff of her citrus scent, he realized he was gaping and blinked. "You can't imagine, but I did win."

"Good for you." She gave him a thumbs-up before turning her attention to the altar, but he couldn't take his eyes off her. She was barely recognizable with her long blond hair falling in soft waves around her shoulders and almost reaching her elbows. Had he ever seen her hair not up in a ponytail? And her sky-blue dress, a far cry from her normal workout wear, brought out the deep blue in her normally slate eyes, and her soft pink lips glistened, plump and—

He jerked his focus to the choir loft, where he caught a glare from Mom and a trip back to his reality. Was he really examining Rainey's lips? Scott loosened his top button in a futile attempt to release the warmth under his collar. He needed to get control of himself.

After the offering, Dad exchanged spots with Henry, who sprinted to the side door, where Rainey's grandmother guided him to children's church. At least Scott wouldn't have to keep apologizing for bumping into Rainey every time he had to stop Henry from fidgeting with the multitude of items stocked in the pew pockets. Whoever thought making pens with springs inside them available to the whim of any little boy obviously hadn't tried to contain Henry for twenty minutes.

The choir rose and waited as the organ introduced the song, and Scott allowed his shoulders to relax, but when he'd catch a glimpse of Rainy's long, slender fingers, or a hint of her sweet scent, his nerves alerted.

"Prone to wander, Lord, I feel it. Prone to leave the God I love," the choir continued, their voices bolder as the melody slowed, and everyone emphasized the words. *"Here's my heart, oh, take and seal it. Seal it for thy courts above."*

That's exactly what he needed to do—seal his heart. Rainey was leaving, and while this friendship could be fun, it had to stop there. He and Dawn had discussed marriage. She'd even thought Henry was cute, but she wouldn't uproot her life. He couldn't expect to have a different result with Rainey. They'd just reconnected, and he'd never ask her to give up her dreams for them. What was he thinking? How had his imagination gone from friends to a long-term relationship in the matter of only a few days?

But this was years in the making. He'd never really gotten over his middle-school crush. He might have shoved his memories of the tall girl with sad slate eyes that occasionally turned blue to the back of his mind, but she'd never left his heart. But it didn't matter. As Henry's guardian, any romantic relationship had to be for the long term. The boy's stability was too important to take chances with, and so a friendship with Rainey would have to be good enough.

Pastor lifted his hands. "Please stand for the closing prayer."

Had he missed the entire sermon? Scott looked around as the congregation stood, and he shot to his feet.

Rainey nudged him. "How was that daydream?"

"I was contemplating the message."

"Sure."

"A-hem." Dad pressed his knuckles to Scott's.

"We're trying something new today." Pastor glanced in Scott and Rainey's direction before switching his attention to the other side of the congregation.

Weird, but he would never be late for church again and get stuck in the front row.

"Everyone join hands and bow your heads," Pastor instructed.

As Scott continued to gawk at Pastor, Dad grabbed his hand. "Stop staring and take the girl's hand."

Scott slipped his now blazing-hot hand around Rainey's,

while his adrenaline spiked like he was down in the count with the bases loaded.

Lord, what are You doing?

Lord, what are You doing? What was happening to her heart? Did it just send shivers through her veins? Was she cold? She didn't think so. Maybe she had a fever, but she wasn't sick, and the only symptom was the unusual ripple in her stomach. Scott was just holding her hand because her grandfather had told him and everyone else to do it. But what was that fragrance? Peppermint and rosemary and—

Rainey, focus. She squeezed her eyes tighter, but Scott's warm hand encompassed hers in the most natural, and at the same time, most disturbing way. Not since their middle-school square dance had she been so overwhelmed with such conflicting emotions. In those days, she'd rejected him on instinct, but this time, she liked how her hand felt in his, like it belonged there.

Too bad Scott would never be interested in her, and she wouldn't even know how to have a romantic relationship. Her experience with men was zero. She'd never even been kissed, and now she was contemplating the possibility of a romance with a man who only wanted to be her friend. But was she reading him right? She had to get out of this place. Had someone turned up the heat?

"Amen," Grandpa said.

"Amen," the congregation responded, and Rainey slid free of Scott's hold and tried to escape, but apparently, Mrs. Saunders, Mrs. Frazier and Mrs. Hopkins had decided this was the best place and time to hold an organizational meeting for a church picnic. The only ways out were to hurdle the rail, crawl over the pew, or navigate around Scott. Thankfully, his dad had left to stand at the church door.

"I hope Henry wasn't too big of a distraction." Scott rocked on his heels. *So relaxed.* Obviously, his nerves weren't on the same racetrack as hers.

"He was fine." Rainey tried for a casual smile, but her cheeks burned like they were the color of the pasta sauce she'd left simmering. "And actually, I need to go. I'm in charge of Sunday dinner." Rainey pointed to the side door. "And you need to get Henry."

"Right." Scott moved into the aisle. "So I'll see you later?"

"Yep." Rainey strode to the parsonage, the winter air prickling her fiery skin. Apparently, fleeing was still the best defense, and she'd have the rest of the day to evaluate and regulate her feelings for Scott.

In her grandmother's kitchen, sunlight poured through the window. Rainey lifted the lid of the cobalt Dutch oven and stirred the sauce. Focusing on the herbs and spices following the spoon, she found her center. Obviously, she'd overreacted, but why? What was it about Scott's hand around hers that had sent her into confusion? It didn't matter; she'd simply make sure it never happened again. She wouldn't end up like her mom, spending years in a melancholy haze after being abandoned by her husband, a man who never supported her dreams. Scott didn't seem like that kind of a man. But how would she know?

Rainey set the spoon on the sunflower spoon rest. Romance and marriage weren't parts of her life plan. She'd made that decision a long time ago, and thankfully, Scott only seemed interested in friendship.

The door flew open, and Grandma hustled inside. "Oh, good, you're here."

"Where else would I be?"

"Who knows? But I would've thought if you had the chance

to chat with a handsome young man, you might take the opportunity."

"If you're referring to Scott, we *chat* almost every day."

"Pish, posh." Grandma waved away Rainey's words. "We
don't have time for this. They're on the way." She snatched
her apron off the hook.

"Who?"

"Scott, Henry and Scott's parents, Judy and Harry." From
the oven, Grandma removed the pan of spaghetti squash that
Rainey had roasted before church and left to keep warm.
"How does this work?"

"I've got it." Rainey grabbed a fork. "We need a large
bowl."

"Knock, knock," a woman's voice called from the front
door. "Ellen? Rainey?"

"We're in the kitchen. Make yourselves at home. I'll be
out in a minute with the iced tea." Grandma grabbed glasses
from the cabinet and placed them on a tray with a pitcher,
while Rainey scraped at the squash's flesh.

"Can I help?" Henry tapped Rainey's arm.

"Only if he won't be in the way." Scott stood behind Henry.

"What a wonderful idea." Grandma lifted the tray. "I'll be
in the living room if you need me."

Rainey pointed at the kitchen table with her elbow. "Grab
a chair for him."

"Here you go." Scott placed the chair beside Rainey.

Henry climbed on the chair. "What's that?"

Scott leaned over Henry, and his cologne or shampoo, or
whatever this new scent was, wafted under Rainey's nose,
making her nerves quiver and her fingers turn to jelly. With
determination, she fisted the fork. "This is spaghetti squash.
See? I'm turning it into noodles, and then we'll put meatballs
and sauce on top."

Henry's forehead bunched. "I don't know."

"Don't be rude," Scott said.

"Do you want to make some spaghetti?" Gaining a measure of composure, Rainey held out a fork to the little boy.

"I guess."

"I'll hold the squash, and you drag the fork through the insides."

Henry did as instructed, scraping out the pulp in strands. "It's amazing! Look, Uncle Scott. I made pasghetti."

Scott chuckled. "You sure did."

"Why don't y'all work on the other half, and I'll finish up these, and then will be ready to eat." Rainey scooted to the side, a warm fuzzy feeling settling inside her. Everything would be okay. It'd probably just been Scott's scent playing tricks on her nerves. She did love rosemary and mint and—she sniffed—lavender, the last ingredient.

After they finished preparing the squash, everyone stood in a circle in the kitchen.

"We're so glad y'all could join us for one of Rainey's amazing meals." Grandpa held out his hands. "Let's say grace."

Positioned between Henry and Grandma, Rainey took their hands, slightly relieved and slightly disappointed not to be holding Scott's. Following the blessing, they made their plates and gathered around the dining-room table.

"Rainey, I can't wait to taste this." Judy lifted her fork. "My boys can't stop talking about your delicious food. I'd love to get your recipes."

"I keep telling her she should start one of those blogs with all her creative dishes. Just the other night she turned okra into Parmesan fries." Grandma cut her meatball. "And her teammates are always messaging her for recipes."

"Grandma, I just like making healthy dishes for my friends and family, and I'm happy to share my recipes. I don't have time to manage a blog." Rainey sipped her tea. After this lunch, she was going for a long run alone. She needed some solitude to recharge.

Grandpa filled his fork. "Henry, how's the soccer going?"

"Great." Henry stabbed a meatball, avoiding the spaghetti squash.

"How are things going with the football field?" Scott asked.

"Well, we don't have to have it ready until the end of April, and with the limited budget, progress is slow."

"It'd be nice to have another field, so the younger kids don't have to share with the high school." Rainey twisted her napkin in her lap. "Honestly, I'm glad the kids are having fun learning the game, but without more field space, soccer doesn't have a chance of getting started here."

"I agree." Scott tapped the edge of his fork against his plate. "Sharing two fields isn't a long-term solution."

"It was fine when you were coming up." Scott's dad raised his brow. "Don't we all think this is just a phase Henry's going through? Surely, he'll decide to play baseball like his dad and uncle."

Scott grimaced. "Not now, Dad."

"I don't disagree with y'all." Grandpa frowned. "We need more fields. And as a matter of fact, about five years ago, the Parkers donated the property adjacent to the elementary school. We'd hoped to create another playing field, but we need to clear it, and sod it, not to mention the cost of upkeep. At a minimum, we need to install irrigation. Unfortunately, there never seems to be any money left in the budget."

"What if we raised the money?" Scott scanned the table. "Maybe we could work with the PTA."

"What are you thinking?" Grandpa leaned in.

"I don't know. How about a softball tournament? When

I was in college, a campus ministry hosted one and made enough money to fund their mission trip."

"Hmm. We could make it an annual event." Grandpa nodded. "It's not a bad idea, but we need someone to organize it."

"I'll do it. Anything to give Henry the chance to play the sport he seems to love." Scott turned to Rainey. "Think you could help me?"

Six sets of eyes landed on Rainey.

"I, uh…" She searched for an excuse. "I don't know the first thing about softball. I'm sure there's a parent who'd be happy to take this on."

"Unlikely. They all have their assignments for the year, and most are burned out." Grandma shook her head. "How about something you do know a lot about?" Grandma tapped her temple. "A cooking competition and cake raffle would be popular. Everyone loves to show off their recipes. Maybe even make a cookbook with the entries."

"That's a fantastic suggestion." Scott's smile widened. "Come on, Rainey. It would be fun. You might even get ideas for recipes."

"I'll think about it." She rose, guilt tugging at her. "Think I'll start the dishes." It was one thing to coach the clinic, where she was still technically getting in touches, but she didn't need another project to take her away from her training.

"I'll help you." Scott shoved the rest of his meal in his mouth, making his cheeks bulge.

"Scott Talmadge Wilcox, where are your manners?" Mrs. Wilcox scowled.

Rainey set her plate in the sink. She hated to let Henry down, but Scott would have to find someone else.

"Sorry. I didn't mean to spring that on you." Scott reached around her with his dishes, his scent enveloping her and awakening a swarm of butterflies in her belly.

"I'm sorry, Scott, but I need to focus on my training."

"I know. I'll do the legwork, I promise. We just make such a good team, and there isn't a lot of time. You're so organized. If you could just help me draw up a plan, like a playbook, I'll handle the rest." Scott folded her hand in his. "Please."

Rainey dropped her gaze to their hands. They did make a good team, and Scott understood her schedule. He understood too much about her. He knew she wanted to help Henry, but she also felt drawn to Scott. When they were working together, life seemed a little easier. It was good to have a friend, and friends supported each other.

"Rainey?" Scott tilted his head, meeting her gaze. "What do you say?"

"Fine, I'll do it for Henry." Straightening to her full height, and in heels that meant almost seeing eye-to-eye with Scott, she clutched his hand. "You owe me big, *Talmadge*."

Chapter Five

With three training sessions completed, the kids arrived for Thursday's practice and warmed up with hardly any instruction. Of course, it helped to have Mindy shouting each exercise. She might be a tad bossy, but Scott would appreciate her help when Rainey was gone.

His stomach knotted. Every day he expected his co-coach to get the *good news* that one of the pro teams had invited her to a tryout. When he couldn't sleep, which was still too often, he'd researched Rainey's career. In college, she'd been a standout, although she hadn't been drafted, but from what he'd learned, it wasn't uncommon for soccer players to go overseas to gain experience playing at a higher level. Rainey had risen in the ranks of the European and Australian leagues. Even with his limited knowledge of professional women's soccer, it seemed she was well on her way to making a team in the National Women's Soccer League and leaving Henry and him behind.

Shaking off his concerns, Scott squared his hips and made his shot. The ball hooked hard left, completely missing the goal…again. "Tell me we're going to practice throws soon."

Mindy smacked her palm to her head. "Coach, you have to hit it with your laces."

"Like this, Uncle Scott." Henry kicked the ball, sending it into the corner of the goal.

"Good job, Henry." Rainey collected the balls and passed them back, never using her hands. She was so talented and kind and helpful and thorough. With Rainey by his side, failing seemed a lot less likely. For good or bad, she'd become a regular part of their days. Whether it was at the twice-a-week soccer clinic, or when she and Scott met to plan the fundraiser and she cooked supper.

At least he could keep Henry in soccer if they got the field ready, and Henry's happiness remained his number-one priority.

"What do you think about those clouds?" Rainey studied the darkening sky.

Scott waved to the parents, chatting at the edge of the field. "Think we better call it." As he helped Rainey grab the balls and cones, a rumble of thunder shook the air. "Henry, get in the jeep!" Scott and Rainey grabbed the equipment bags, dashed across the field and closed their doors as the clouds unloaded.

Once they arrived at the house, Rainey prepared supper while Scott got Henry in the bath. With shampoo lathered on Henry's head, Scott hurried to the kitchen for a cup. Why didn't he just leave one in the bathroom? It seemed simple enough. By now, he should have gotten bath time down, but until recently, it'd been a struggle.

Scott rushed to the cupboard, but out of the corner of his eye, he glimpsed the color drain from Rainey's face as she gaped at her phone.

"Everything okay?"

"Oh, yes." She pocketed the phone and stirred the meat. "Forget the cup again?"

"Yep, but I'm leaving it in there tonight."

"Good plan," she said flatly before worrying her lip. What had happened? She'd been fine on the drive.

"Rainey, are you sure—"

"Uncle Scott!" Henry screamed, but Rainey didn't react at all, she just kept stirring.

"I'm coming." The hairs on the back of his neck alerted, but he'd have to wait to talk to her. He couldn't risk shampoo dripping into Henry's eyes.

An hour later, Scott closed Henry's door. "Thank You, God." Every night, the routine worked a little better, and he owed it all to Rainey's advice. What Henry needed most was consistency.

At the dining-room table, Rainey slumped over her cell phone. She typed something, frowned and then tapped repeatedly, likely deleting the message. She'd been distracted during supper and didn't notice him now. Maybe she didn't know how to tell him that she'd be leaving soon. He dragged his fingers through his hair, stopping at the back of his head and kneading out the tension. If he wasn't such a wimp, he'd just ask her, but would living in the bliss of ignorance one more night really hurt?

Scott pulled out the chair beside her and sat.

Rainey startled and placed her phone on the notebook in front of her. "Ready to work?" She snatched two parts of her hair and tightened her ponytail with what could only be described as feigned enthusiasm as she strained to hold up the corners of her mouth. "What's first?"

This was not the expression of someone who'd recently heard all her dreams were about to come true. Something was wrong. Scott's chest no longer felt weighed down, but lifted with hope. He was so selfish. He should be concerned, but if Rainey was disappointed, it meant she wasn't leaving…yet.

"First, tell me what's wrong."

"I don't know what you mean. I'm great." The edges of her lips stretched across her reddening face.

"Yeah, I don't think so. I knew something was up when you let the water boil over." He touched her cheek. "Please stop making that face. You look like the Joker."

Rainey smacked his hand. "Wow, you sure know how to charm a girl."

"Thought my powers were lost on you."

"Ha ha." She rocked back in her seat.

"Seriously, what's got the most focused person I know flustered?"

"I am not flustered. I don't think I've ever been flustered."

"We both know that's not true." He smirked.

"You're terrible." She glared at him. "And I think you can handle this on your own." She pressed her palms against the table like she was about to stand.

"Wait. I'm sorry." Scott grasped her wrist. "I was kidding. I do need you. Please stay."

"Fine." Rainey slipped free of his hold, folding her arms over her middle.

"Seriously, what's wrong?"

"My dad's getting married." She huffed.

"And that's a bad thing?"

"It is when he's marrying your favorite coach who's less than ten years older than you, and he's doing it in two weeks." She rolled her head to meet his gaze.

What should he say? He didn't want to make things worse with his opinion of her dad and coach's thoughtless actions, but he had to say something.

"Wow. That's a lot." Scott nodded, clenching his jaw.

"No kidding." Rainey massaged her temples. She didn't need him to fight for her—she needed him to listen.

"Have they been together long?"

"Not really. That's why I came here for my break." She braided her fingers under her chin. "I thought it was just a fling. Dad hasn't been in a serious relationship since the divorce."

"And she was your coach?"

"From my junior year of high school and during breaks while I was in college. I've trained with Kayce for almost ten years. She's still sending me workouts. Until now, I've been able to compartmentalize our relationship."

"Rainey, I'm so sorry. Don't they understand how this kind of distraction can affect your game? Couldn't they wait until after your tryout?" His pulse pounded as he gave in to his outrage. He hated the idea of Rainey leaving, but this was her dream. How could her own father, not to mention her coach, be so selfish?

"In his text, Dad said they wanted to get married on Valentine's Day." Rainey sighed.

"Text?" Scott snapped.

"Did I forget to mention that sweet detail? Yep, my supersensitive father couldn't be bothered to pick up a phone and call his only child with his *big* news."

"Yikes. I thought y'all might be closer, since he was the one who got you into soccer."

"We have a professional relationship."

"How so?"

"He's my agent. Honestly, if it weren't for my career, we probably wouldn't have any relationship." Rainey shrugged. "He basically abandoned me and my mom when he graduated from law school. That's when we moved here."

"I'm sorry. I didn't know." Scott's abdominal muscles tightened. Poor Rainey, the tall, thin girl with large almond-shaped eyes that changed color in a way that intrigued him. She'd been dealing with so much, and all he could think of at twelve years old was getting her attention and then that stupid dare. "And we didn't give you the warmest welcome."

She shot him a look that said he'd definitely understated the situation.

"I feel terrible. What can I say? We were stupid kids." His pulse ticked up. He should tell her what a mess she'd made him.

"Hank was nice," she said.

"That's the kind of guy he was." Scott took a long slow breath. "Can I make a confession?"

"You're not going to try to one-up me, are you?" She quirked her head. "Because I'm really enjoying rehashing my sad past."

"I'm pretty sure we tie for sad stories." It was now or never. He tucked his chin, avoiding her gaze. "I had the biggest crush on you."

"What? You teased me mercilessly." She playfully popped his bicep.

Scott cringed. "I didn't know how else to get you to notice me."

"I don't believe you."

"I promise." He placed his hand over his heart.

"No, I believe that you had a crush on me." Rainey snickered. "I can't believe you told me."

"You seemed like you needed a laugh."

"That square-dance incident has haunted me my entire life. I can barely listen to country music."

"I'm the one who got the broken arm."

"I still feel bad about that." Rainey wrinkled her nose in that way that made him want to kiss the tip of it. Whoa, he better stifle that impulse. The last time he'd given in to a desire to kiss her, things hadn't ended well.

"Don't. I deserved it."

"Maybe." She burst into giggles.

"I'm glad you're finding such amusement in my tragic story." But her laughter sent a river of warm ripples through him like nothing he'd experienced, and he didn't want it to stop.

"Tragic story, you're hilarious." She chuckled. "I'd heard some guys talking about the kissing dare, and when you leaned in, I just reacted. I didn't mean to do-si-do you into the gym wall."

"Interesting, because as I was soaring through the air, it definitely felt intentional."

Rainey stopped laughing and stared him right in the eyes. "Truly, I'm sorry." She rolled her lips together, but a few giggles escaped.

"You aren't, but it's fine. And just so you know it wasn't only about the dare for me." He pushed himself from the table before all this talk of kissing made his heart beat out of his chest. This friendship was becoming harder and harder to manage. "I'm getting a glass of water. You want anything?"

"Scott, don't be mad." Rainey bit down on her lip.

Look away, Scott. Look away.

"I'm not, really." He darted to the kitchen. "Just thirsty." He ripped open the freezer door and stuck his head inside. If she only knew how much stronger his feelings for her were now than they were then. He rolled his shoulders like he'd always done before he batted and then grabbed a tray of ice.

"Thank you," Rainey said.

He jumped and dropped the tray.

"Sorry, I didn't mean to startle you." She bent and picked up the tray and the cubes that had fallen out.

"It's fine. I just didn't hear you." Scott's pulse raced like he'd run ten laps around the bases, or at least that's what he thought it'd feel like. He carried another tray to the sink and placed ice in the glasses. "What are you thanking me for?"

"Taking my mind off Dad and Kayce. Making me laugh. I didn't realize how upset I was. And also, I don't know, it feels better knowing you weren't making fun of me."

"I'm sorry I made you feel that way, and I'm glad I could help now, but it feels like an apology isn't enough." He sipped the cold water, calming his nerves.

"Actually, it goes a long way, but I'm sure I can think of some other way for you to make it up to me."

"I already owe you so much."

"And don't think I'm not keeping track," she teased, but her expression faltered. "I still need to respond to the happy couple and tell my mom."

"How will she take the news?" Scott reclined against the counter.

"Better than me. It's been a long time, and she's living her best life these days."

"Really?"

"After we left here, we moved to the coast, and she kept teaching. She'd supported our family while my dad was in law school. Unfortunately, he found that his study partners were good for more than trading notes, if you know what I mean. I think Mom would've stayed with him, but he wanted to keep making new *friends*, so he remained in Jacksonville. Anyway, after I graduated from high school, my mom became a flight attendant."

"What?"

Rainey flipped her palm in the air. "She said it'd always been her dream."

"That's great."

"Yeah, she's really happy." Rainey nodded. "Still, I think she'd like to hear about the impending wedding from me. I didn't tell her about Dad and Kayce's change of relationship status because I thought it would end quickly, but she does follow Kayce on social media. Although Kayce rarely posts, I'm sure she'll post some pics of her wedding, and I don't want Mom to find out about it from a picture of me standing next to Kayce holding a bouquet."

"Come again?"

"Oh, did I forget to tell you the best part? Kayce wants me to be her maid of honor."

"And?" It seemed like cruel and unusual punishment to him.

"I don't think I have a choice." She frowned. "The worst part is I'll end up sitting by myself all night. You may have noticed I'm not a big fan of strangers or small talk."

"You don't say." He cocked a brow. "What if I went with you? I do owe you a lot." He dropped in air quotes, trying to seem playful even though going to a wedding with Rainey wasn't exactly in the safety zone he was trying to maintain, but he wanted her to be happy.

"Are you serious?" Rainey touched her cheek.

"I'll even take a chance and dance with you." He lifted his arms like he was holding a dance partner and sashayed in a circle as his heart did its own irritating jig. "It'll be fun." He stopped in front of her. "What do you say?"

"This is seriously one of the nicest things anyone has ever done for me." Rainey caught her bottom lip in her teeth, her eyes glistening with unshed tears.

"If that's true, you need better friends." Scott pulled her into a hug. If he kept repeating the word, maybe his brain could convince his heart it was true.

Following another late-night planning session with Scott and thankfully a few parent volunteers, Rainey had allowed herself to sleep in. At least in her dreams, she could play pro soccer and leap into Scott's arms when she scored a goal. He'd been so supportive and patient when she'd needed to vent about Dad and Kayce. Even if she and Scott were just friends, she valued their relationship, and she was filled with relief knowing she'd have someone on her team at the wedding.

Instead of her predawn run, Rainey tried a new spinach, egg and quinoa recipe followed by a challenging online yoga class. Then she ran out to the country and back to the high school, where her hamstring cramped mercilessly, but she still needed to work out her upper body.

Entering the weight room, Rainey inhaled the solitude that helped her focus. During this time of day, Scott taught middle-school classes. Being the baseball coach and teaching the high-school and middle-school PE classes really was a lot for a guy learning how to be a single dad, but he kept giving himself more responsibilities, like the fundraiser.

With her leg extended in front of her, Rainey slowly bent until her fingertips touched the floor. Her taut hamstring strained against the stretch, but she held the position, inhaling deep breaths, sending oxygen to her tense muscles. This pain would all be worth it. Exhaling, she deepened the stretch, pressing her palms into the mat.

"Just the girl I was hoping for." Scott's voice broke her concentration.

"I'm sure you can find someone else."

"Please, will you help me out? It'll only take a few minutes. Fifteen max." Scott clasped his hands in front of his face. "Please. I'll be your best friend."

"I'd rather have ice cream with strawberries on top." She shook out her leg.

"That can be arranged if my friendship isn't enough."

"What do you need?"

He held out his hand. "An assistant."

"I'm going to need two scoops." She slapped his palm as she brushed by him.

"Whatever you want."

"Isn't leaving the kids unsupervised frowned upon?"

"Mrs. Mayfield is with them." He held the door.

As she entered the gym, Rainey looked over her shoulder. "So why do you need an assistant?"

"She's serving as the DJ—" he grinned, a mischievous glint in his eyes "—and caller."

Rainey spun around. The students sat in boy-girl pairs in squares on the gym floor.

"Oh, no." Rainey pivoted but ran smack into Scott as her body was engulfed in an inferno of humiliation.

"Please, give me a chance." Scott held her arms as she tried to wiggle away. "It'll be fun. Besides it'll be good practice for the wedding reception."

"I doubt there will be square dancing at a beach wedding." She had to get out of here. Her pulse pounded hard as her lungs constricted. "I can't." She pressed her palms into his chest, her knees wobbling.

"Take a deep breath." He squeezed her arms gently. "I'm sorry I didn't realize."

"I know," she said on a heavy breath as the wave of trembles crested and began to recede.

Taking a step back, Scott slid his palms down her arms to hold her hands. "I thought we could replace a bad memory with a good one." He peered into her eyes with a steadying resolve.

As she focused on her reflection in his nearly black eyes, her pulse steadied. She didn't need to do this, but maybe she should.

"Just don't try anything extra. I can still send you flying."

With her nerves still skittering, she gave him a curt nod. *Fake it 'til you make it.*

"Never doubted it." Relief spread across his face, and he perused the room behind her. "What are y'all staring at? Everyone stand up." He held her hand firmly, guiding her to one of the squares. "Alright, boys hold your hands out, girls set yours on top. This is the starting position and place we will come back to." Scott demonstrated with Rainey. "If you get confused, just watch us."

Instead of following Scott's directions, the kids squealed and squirmed.

A girl with braided hair smacked her partner's knuckles. "Jack's mashing my hand."

"McKenna will only give me one finger." The boy next to Rainey tilted his head at the girl next to him, who simply shrugged but placed a second finger on his palm.

"Will I get a bad grade if Aaron trips and makes us fall?" a girl whined.

"Y'all be quiet." Scott clapped. "We are all in this together."

Rainey giggled, and Scott glared at her. "Not you, too."

"Sorry. What's next?" Rainey turned to the girl beside her. "Is he always this bossy?"

All the nearby kids nodded.

"Everyone, listen to Mrs. Mayfield. She'll call out the directions. We'll practice without music first, so no one gets confused or trips." He winked at Rainey. "We don't want anyone to get hurt."

"Very funny." Rainey rolled her eyes.

"Glad to see you trying to fit in with the seventh graders."

"First, we'll try the do-si-do," Mrs. Mayfield said. "Y'all will like this one. You don't have to hold hands. Everyone face your partner. Now, walk around, passing right shoulders. Ready? Go."

"This isn't as bad as I remember." Rainey stepped past Scott. "I'm glad—"

"Aaron ran into me. Coach Wilcox, I told you I needed a different partner."

"Julie, you don't need another partner. Just try again."

And they did, but after twenty minutes and only two more moves, the bell rang, and the kids cleared the room in what Rainey would guess was a record-setting pace with Mrs. Mayfield chasing after them to slow down.

As the gym door banged shut, Rainey fell into Scott's side. "I can't believe they are still teaching this."

"It's the principal's mandate, so I don't have a choice." He gave her a side hug. "Thanks for helping. I'm sorry I caught you off guard."

"Just don't forget my payment." She headed for the door. "See you later."

"Think you could help tomorrow?"

"Actually, I think I can." She continued into the hall, her palms still warm from holding his hands. Yes, she could spare half an hour for the comfort of his touch even if he only considered her a friend.

Chapter Six

❧

Slapping on his ball cap, Scott rushed from the school building. How had he let time get away from him? He'd planned to apologize again to Rainey before the kids arrived for soccer practice, but he'd have to make it up to her with an extra topping on her ice-cream sundae. For someone who took her nutrition so seriously, he was surprised she'd requested such a decadent treat. He'd have to tease her about it later.

Later.

How much more time did they really have before she was training with a professional soccer team and too busy for a visit? He'd checked the schedule for the National Women's Soccer League, and preseason practices started in March. As he understood the plan, her dad was working on getting her a tryout during that time.

Scott stopped at the edge of the field and shoved away the sinking feeling. Across the outfield, Rainey's blond ponytail bounced as she jogged beside the kids warming up. He wanted her to have her dream. Of all people, he understood what it meant to work hard and make it professionally, but he loved having her around.

Wait. Loved? He squeezed his eyes shut. *Man, you are a mess.*

As he opened his eyes, a soccer ball ricocheted off the

grass and shot toward his face. He threw up his hands and caught it. "Nice shot."

"You're late," Rainey shouted. "Think you could meditate later and help me with these kids?"

"Sorry." He tossed her the ball. "What can I do?"

"Set up the cones in two lines." Rainey turned back to the kids. "We're going to practice dribbling. Everyone get a ball and get in a line before I count to five."

As she counted, the kids dashed to their lines. "Nice trick." Scott placed the last cone. She was really good with the kids, always coming up with ways to manage them but still have fun.

"You're welcome to borrow it. I'll warn you it works best when they know there is a potential reward." She pointed to a cooler. "I baked cookies."

"First ice cream and now, cookies. Are you feeling alright?"

"Oatmeal cookies, and what can I say? I love ice cream, so I splurge once in a while, especially if someone else is buying." She twirled away from him. "Alright, everyone watch me." With the insides of her feet, Rainey touched a ball slowly as she threaded the cones.

For the rest of the session, the kids practiced dribbling the ball through various drills. Scott was surprised at how quickly they learned, especially since he kept tripping over the ball or his own feet.

Henry dribbled by him. "You've almost got it, Uncle Scott."

"I guess it's hard to teach an old dog new tricks." Rainey kicked her ball in circles around him.

Scott snatched up the soccer ball. "No doubt I can teach you how to hit a baseball."

"Maybe someday." Rainey jogged to the cooler and retrieved a plastic box. "Great practice. You each earned one cookie."

Scott joined her as the last kid marched through the gate. "Why wait for someday?" He hitched his thumb toward the batting cage.

"It's getting dark, and I can't have another late night."

"Come on, I'll take you for that ice-cream sundae afterward." He closed the gate. "My parents are picking up Henry for supper and will bring him home. I promise I'll have you back to your grandparents' house before you turn into Cinderella."

"I don't think that's how the story goes, and I'm pretty sure her moment of truth occurred at midnight, so—"

"Fine, how's eight sound?"

"You really think you can teach me how to hit a baseball and get me ice cream by eight o'clock?" She raised her eyebrows almost to her headband.

"Before eight o'clock." Scott galloped backward. "Just got to switch on the lights and get a bat. Meet me at the batting cage when you finish cleaning up."

"Thanks for the help," Rainey yelled after him.

Adrenaline coursed through him as he reached the field house and hit the switch for the field lights. He selected a couple of bats that he'd use for the middle-school session on baseball if they ever got through this square-dance unit.

With the bats resting on his shoulder and the tremors of nerves settling, Scott entered the batting cage. He left the bats on the plate and crossed to the pitching machine.

Rainey dropped her equipment bag. "Let's get this over with so I can have my ice cream."

"Don't sound so excited." Scott removed the cover from the pitching machine.

"We aren't using that, are we?" Rainey pointed. "It doesn't look safe."

"It's perfectly safe, and we may not even use it." He strode toward her. "Grab a bat."

"If you say so." Rainey kept one eye fixed on the machine as she bent for a bat.

Scott lifted the other bat. "First, hold the end like this, lining up your knuckles." He demonstrated.

"Like this?"

"Perfect."

"Okay, what's next?"

"Hover the bat above your shoulder, widen your stance and bend your knees." He checked her stance. "Good. Now, plant your back foot, and as you swing the bat around your body, shift your weight forward and take a small step with your front foot."

"Like this?" She swung slowly, more like a robot than a batter.

"You've got to loosen up. It's more like dance—"

"Do you really want to finish that sentence?" She pointed the end of the bat at him.

"Right." He held up a hand in surrender. "Try shaking your arms loose and watch me." Scott swung the bat slowly but smoothly. "Give it another go."

Rainey wiggled her arms like they were noodles and then gripped the end of the bat. She swung hard and the bat slipped from her fingers, flying into the net. "Oops." She grimaced. "Guess it is like square dancing…with you, anyway."

"I'm going to ignore that comment." Scott retrieved Rainey's bat. "You're getting the hang of it. I'm going to toss some balls to you and just try to make contact." He grabbed a ball from a bucket. "Ready?"

"I guess." Rainey pulled back the bat.

"Just keep your eye on the ball." Scott threw it to her, aiming for where she would swing. He'd learned from his brother that sometimes it was easier for the coach to hit the bat than a new player to hit the ball, but Rainey swung too late, and the ball sailed by her. Scott held up another ball. "Swing a little faster this time."

But, of course, she zipped the bat around too fast and missed again. This would require a more hands-on approach.

"Do a few more practice swings, while I switch on the machine."

"I don't think I'm ready for the machine."

"Neither do I, so I'm going to help you get the feel of it. Don't worry. It'll be on the slowest setting."

Trekking to the machine, he inhaled as all his nerve endings jumped to attention. They'd be in close contact—very close contact—but he could handle it. Scott released what breath he could as he switched on the machine. Maybe the whir of the motor would drown out his thumping heart.

Scott stepped behind Rainey as a ball floated by them. "I'm going to put my hands around yours, okay?"

"Mmm-hmm." Her knuckles whitened as she squeezed the bat.

Scott encircled her shoulders and covered her hands with his, trying to keep his body from brushing hers. But her ponytail tickled his cheek, and a whiff of citrus delighted his senses.

"Scott?" Rainey turned her head, their noses nearly touching. As she searched his eyes, his resolve melted into the depths of her gaze. The colors of her eyes swirled to create the slate blue that he seemed unable to drag his focus from until her breath brushed against his lips, drawing him closer.

"Rainey." He cupped her head.

Her eyes grew wide like she was...*afraid*?

His heart slammed against his ribs.

* * *

"I have to go." Rainey jerked free of him and ducked as a ball flew above her head. Was he going to kiss her? Was she going to kiss him? Her pulse pounded as she stumbled from the cage and sprinted across the field. The cool air stung her hot cheeks, defeating the momentary flutters of her heart. At the parsonage gate, she finally slowed her pace and risked a glance over her shoulder. The lights from the baseball field glowed warm in the dark night. Shivering, she rubbed her arms, missing Scott's embrace, but she couldn't. She didn't even know how, and even if she did, it would ruin everything.

The lights cut off, leaving nothing but the sliver of a crescent moon on a black sky. Rainey exhaled a long, slow breath. What must he be thinking?

What if he was only trying to get her attention? If only she had a little experience with guys, his cues—if they even were cues—wouldn't be so hard to read. She trudged to the house. At least she could be alone. Her grandparents wouldn't be home from church for a while.

Inside, Rainey collapsed on the couch and flipped on the television to watch the national team and get her mind off Scott. For that matter, she needed to focus on her game if she ever hoped to play on this team. All this small-town charm had distracted her, especially the baseball coach and his adorable nephew. Her chest clenched, and she increased the volume. The crowd cheered as the team ran onto the field and got into formation. Rainey leaned forward, clutching her hands under her chin, concentrating on each pass as if she was on the pitch.

At the forty-second minute, a tapping on the window behind the couch startled her, and she spun around. Scott waved, and Rainey's stomach dropped. Why hadn't she drawn the curtains?

As she turned the doorknob, a whistle squealed from the

television, fraying her last semblance of composure, and she jerked the door open.

"You okay?" Scott gave her a puzzled look as he lowered a paper cup with a plastic dome over what appeared to be a rather large, well-adorned ice-cream sundae.

"Fine." But her stomach protested with a loud grumble.

The corners of Scott's lips quirked up in that most irritatingly cute grin, and Rainey's heart did a flip, leaving her searching for something to say.

"Can I come in? I did bring your payment, and from the sounds of it, you might be hungry."

"You can come in, but only because I want that ice cream." Rainey crossed to the couch, holding her stomach so the butterflies might get the message.

"Whatever it takes." Scott closed the door. "Important game?" He gave her a plastic spoon and her sundae, but best of all, an excuse for her hasty departure.

With her pulse finally settling, Rainey pried off the lid. "Sorry, I forgot about it earlier, and I needed to study this game. It's part of an international tournament for the national women's team. These are some of the best players. They all play on professional teams, some in the States and some in Europe, but play together for the US. This tournament is a lead-up for the World Cup qualifiers. It's halftime." With nothing left from her arsenal of national-team updates, besides listing all the players and their professional teams, which she might resort to later if she needed to direct the conversation away from her weird behavior or anything about their relationship, Rainey shoved an oversized bite in her mouth.

A commentator's voice blared from the television speakers, describing an earlier goal.

Scott winced. "Wow, he's excited. Do you mind if I turn it down?"

"Sure, sorry. I wanted the in-person experience. You know, with the cheering fans."

Scott lifted the remote and lowered the volume. "I'm glad you remembered the game. I was worried that, uh, that I scared you off with the pitching machine."

"Nope. Just the game." Rainey tunneled her spoon through the layers of ice cream and toppings, ignoring her trotting pulse. "My dad will make sure I watched." At least he usually checked in with her, and they discussed the games. Sometimes he even called during halftime. Those conversations were pretty much the only times he called, but with the wedding less than two weeks away, he might not bother.

"When's the next game?" Scott pointed his spoon at the screen.

"Saturday afternoon."

"Maybe we could watch it together. Henry would love having you explain everything."

"Sure. I really like spending time with him." *And you*. But she didn't dare look up from her next spoonful. "He gets so excited." She placed the creamy mixture in her mouth, enjoying how the sugar and caramel blended together.

"Yeah, it's nice to be someone's hero." Scott plunged his spoon into his bowl.

"I didn't mean it like that. I didn't even mean for that to happen. I hope I'm not messing up things for y'all. That's the last thing—"

"You're the only reason we have any sort of a relationship, so I'll take what I can get."

"Okay." But he sounded far from fine, and she didn't know how else to help him.

"Rainey, I really do appreciate all you're doing for Henry, and well, for me. I know it's a sacrifice—"

"It's no problem. We're friends." Out of the corner of her eye, she saw the players take the field.

"Okay, but—"

The referee's whistle blew—perfect timing.

"Sorry, the second half is starting." Rainey shifted, squaring her body to face the TV and end this conversation. "You want to stay?"

"Actually, I better go. Henry will be home soon." Scott moved to the door.

"See you tomorrow." Rainey focused on the screen like her life depended on it, and maybe it did in a way. Finally, the door clicked shut, and she let her body relax into the cushions. So much had been left unsaid, but all those words would make things more complicated…and more difficult for her to leave.

Chapter Seven

After dropping off Henry and Champ with his parents, Scott drove to the parsonage. The past week and a half was a blur, and he hadn't had more than a few minutes alone with Rainey. She'd increased her workouts and never seemed to be in the weight room when he took breaks. When they were together, she acted like nothing had happened, and really, nothing had happened. Even if he wanted more with Rainey, it was impossible. He wanted her to be happy, and being her friend through this wedding was the best way to do that…*as her friend*.

As Scott exited the jeep, Mrs. Ellen approached him. "You're so sweet to take Rainey to her dad's wedding. I don't suppose I need to tell you she's wound up like a jack-in-the-box."

"I'm not surprised. She told me about her relationship with her dad and Kayce."

"I figured as much, so I'm going to tell you some things about Rainey that I'm certain she hasn't told you."

"Okay." Scott closed his door.

"She's never dated, and when I say never, I don't mean like Pastor never speeds. I mean *never*." She shook her head slowly. "So if she seems awkward when y'all are together, she's trying to figure everything out, and trust me, that critical voice in her head is giving her terrible advice."

"Wow, I didn't realize." But it explained so much and yet nothing at all. His temperature rose as he tried to keep his composure.

"Exactly why I'm telling you." She glanced over her shoulder. "I know you don't want to get in the way of her career because you know better than anyone how important it is to her, but at some point, she'll want a husband and a family—"

"Whoa." Scott waved his hands. "Let's not get ahead of ourselves. I'm glad you told me about Rainey's dating history, or lack of it, but we're just friends. She's made that very clear."

"Don't you understand?" Mrs. Ellen squinted at him like he was out of focus. "She doesn't know how to take the next step even if she wanted to. If you want more, and I think you do, you're going to have to pitch the ball, swing the bat and call the strikes."

"Interesting metaphor, but I get you. Still, even if I did want more with Rainey, this isn't the right time for us." He ran his fingers through his hair. "She's leaving in a few weeks, maybe even less, and I need to focus on Henry, and apparently, raising money for the school district's athletic department."

"All I'm saying is there's never a perfect time for love." Mrs. Ellen pivoted. "You coming?" She hustled to the house. Maybe he should make a run for it before Mrs. Ellen had them at the altar with Pastor.

"Scott," Mrs. Ellen said in her teacher voice.

"Yes, ma'am." He hurried after her, entering the house.

"You didn't need to come inside." Rainey gave him a tentative smile, looking between her grandmother and Scott.

Mrs. Ellen moved to the side. "A gentleman always collects his date inside. What would you have him do, honk the horn like some barbarian?"

"I'm not his date." Rainey slung her duffel over her shoulder and picked up a garment bag. "Scott is doing me a favor as a *friend*."

"Call it what you like." Mrs. Ellen pecked Rainey's cheek. "Y'all have fun. Love you."

Scott hooked his finger under the exposed hangers. "At least let me take that before she tells my mother I need manners lessons."

"Thanks." She turned to the rear of the house. "Grandpa, we're leaving."

"Be careful on the roads, Scott." Pastor entered the room. "You never know when a deer will decide it's a good time to go for a stroll."

"Yes, sir." His chest tensed, the elephant suddenly very present in the room.

Pastor hugged Rainey. "I'll be praying for you, honey."

"We'll be praying for all of you." Mrs. Ellen patted his back.

"Thanks," Scott managed to say before his throat thickened, and he exited the house.

"We'll let you know when we get there." Rainey quickened her pace to match his until they stopped behind the jeep. "Sorry about all that. What was Grandma telling you?"

"Trust me. You don't want the details. Let's just say she wants you to be happy and leave it at that." He positioned the bag across the back seat.

She tossed her duffel in the cargo area. "Oh, no. I'm so embarrassed."

"Don't be. She cares about you." He held her door.

"How long are you going to keep up this gentleman routine?"

"I don't know what you're talking about. I'm always a gentleman." He closed her door and rounded the front of the jeep.

When he joined her, she said, "Thanks again for going

with me. I don't know what to expect, and it'll really be nice to have someone there on my team."

He started the vehicle and reversed. "Funny you should say that. I was thinking about how we make a great team."

"Yes, you've mentioned that, but it always ends with me working on some project with you. At least this time, you're doing something for me."

He chuckled. "I'm happy to be on a team with you anytime, and we can use it to our advantage."

"Now, you have my attention. Tell me more."

"We're both used to playing sports, so what if we approach this wedding like a big game?"

"Interesting. We could come up with plays and signals."

"Right. If you need me to come in to take a pass, you tuck your hair behind your left ear."

Rainey giggled.

"What?" He glanced at her.

"I'm just picturing me tossing you a piece of wedding cake after I see you touch your nose once, tug your ear twice and pat your shoulder." She demonstrated the signal.

Laughing with her, he turned onto the long stretch of two-lane highway that threaded the endless fields of pine trees as the setting sun threw shadows across the gray road in front of them. While they continued to develop their playbook, the awkwardness that had resided between them since the batting-cage incident faded and their easy friendship returned.

As they traversed the causeway to St. Simons Island, moonlight shimmered on the dark rivers carving through the marsh. Rainey focused on breathing exercises, but her pulse seemed unwilling to decrease. After they'd devised several signals, they'd driven in a comfortable silence. Scott seemed to have a lot on his mind, and while she wanted to help him, her grandmother's insinuation that this was a date stopped her. Besides, she had her own set of issues to grapple with and pray over. For most of her life, playing soccer at the highest level had been her primary focus. She'd never been distracted from her goal, but Scott and Henry made her aware of all kinds of emotions and thoughts she'd never considered.

Rainey closed her eyes. *Lord, help me find my way.*

Scott touched her arm. "How are you doing?"

"My nerves are on high alert, but otherwise I'm fine." She rolled her phone in her hand, wishing she had a ball and time to kick it around. "I'm not sure what to expect. Dad asked me to meet them in the lobby when I arrived."

"Do you want me to come with you?"

"Yes, but I better do this on my own."

"I'll keep my phone close by, so you can call if you need to." He steered through a roundabout. "Is this the first time you've seen them together?"

"Yes. Ever since he mentioned they were dating, I've avoided them. It wasn't hard when I was overseas. I thought it'd be over before I had to deal with them in person."

"At least you'll be able to put it behind you after tomorrow and focus on your tryout." Scott drove through the stoplight in the village. It was quiet for a Friday night, but it was the middle of winter. Not exactly tourist season at the beach, which was why they'd probably been able to book everything so quickly.

"This is where you grew up, right?" Scott asked as they passed St. Simons Elementary School. "Did you go to school there?"

"Yes. It was great. We could walk to the beach for picnics and science lessons." She pointed. "Turn here, and we'll be able to see the ocean."

Scott followed her directions and braked as the vast, dark

sea came into view. When the waves crashed on the shore, white foam exploded in the moonlight.

"Tide must be coming in," she said.

"Do you miss living by the ocean?" He continued down the street.

"I rarely got to enjoy it when I was here. We were always driving back and forth to Jacksonville for practices and games. It'd be nice to visit as a tourist."

"We're definitely not leaving until we go for a walk on the beach." At the King and Prince Hotel, Scott parked under the porte cochere.

"We could go now." She gestured toward the beach access.

"Nice try, but you'll feel better after you talk to them. Remember, you have a special relationship with Kayce, and as far as you know, she's still the coach you loved. Give her a chance."

"You're right."

"But it doesn't make it any easier." Scott opened his door. "I'll get us checked in."

"Thanks. I'm so glad you're here. I'll text when we finish talking." She ambled into the lobby, perusing the space. Soft music played from a hidden speaker, while flames danced in the large stone fireplace. With the dark wood floors and the warm glow from the chandeliers that hung from wood beams, the room felt more like a large living room than a hotel lobby. As she passed behind a couch, a couple snuggled, sharing an intimate conversation. Her chest squeezed hard, fighting the waves in her stomach. Something like that with someone she could tell her innermost thoughts would be nice…someday, just not today or even tomorrow.

At the edge of the dining room, she stopped and rolled her shoulders. Dad and Kayce, and his arm was draped around her. Kayce saw Rainey first and smiled, waving as Dad rose.

Before she could reach the table, Dad wrapped her in a hug. "Thank you for coming." He pressed a kiss to the top of her head. What was going on? In the past, Dad's most expressive gesture was a high-five after a game. Otherwise, he was hands-off.

Rainey retreated from his embrace to find Kayce gathering her in her arms. "Can you believe this? It's so wonderful. My favorite player will now be part of my family." At least she hadn't said *stepdaughter*. Rainey's skin prickled against the increasing awkwardness of their situation.

"Let's sit down. We have so much to tell you." Dad pulled out a chair for her. "Have you eaten? Do you want something to drink? Will your friend be joining us?"

"Give her a chance to answer, honey." Kayce squeezed his shoulder.

Did Kayce call Dad honey? "Um, I—" Rainey gaped at them. She tried to get her feet to move, but it was like they'd sunk into wet sand. If only she could tuck her hair behind her ear and Scott was nearby, so he could get her signal.

"Rainey, are you okay?" A hand pressed into her back, and Scott's scent drew her attention. Had he been wearing that all day? He stepped in front of her, peering into her eyes. "I wanted to give you your keycard. Do you need me to stay?"

Rainey tucked her hair behind her ear. "Just for a minute."

Scott extended his hand. "Hi, I'm Scott Wilcox. You must be Rainey's dad and Kayce, the world's best soccer coach."

"Yes, I'm John Allen," Dad said.

While they all made introductions, Rainey retreated from the circle. Scott was so charming. No wonder everyone loved him. He made people feel at ease and important. He made her feel at ease and important. She could do this.

"I'll take our luggage up to the rooms, but I'd love to join y'all for dinner if Rainey is up for it." Apparently, they'd been making plans while she centered herself. Scott slid the chair farther from the table. With one hand on her arm and the other on her back, he guided her into the seat. "You've got this," he whispered, his warm breath prickling her neck.

"We'll see you soon." Dad clapped Scott's shoulder in a move that almost seemed like he was asserting himself between them. Was he being protective?

"Of course. I'll hurry." Scott gave Rainey a knowing look before he left the table.

"What a great guy, Rainey." Kayce settled her attention on Rainey. "How did y'all meet?"

"We were in the same PE class in middle school. Scott was my square-dance partner." Rainey switched her attention to the man impersonating her father, years of bitterness refusing to be subdued. "Yeah, it was the year Mom and I lived in Woodley, while you frolicked in the big city, and our worlds crumbled. But you wouldn't know about any of that, would you?" Her pulse pounded in her ears. Scott was wrong. She did not have this. She was not like him.

"Rainey, I'm so sorry for what I did to you and Cynthia. I was selfish and impulsive." He placed his hand on her back. "I'm sorry I hurt you. I know it's a lot to ask, but will you forgive me? I want to have a relationship with you. I want to be more than your agent. I want to be…your—" his voice broke, and he cleared his throat "—dad."

Rainey swallowed, making room to release the breath that felt trapped by her constricted lungs. She pressed her eyes closed, squeezing them tightly until finally her chest relaxed, and she exhaled, opening her eyes. "I don't know what to say. I don't even understand."

"Rainey, your dad is asking you for a second chance. Here, let me—" With a napkin, Kayce reached for Rainey's face, but Rainey flinched away.

"I got that much." Rainey snatched the napkin from Kayce and wiped away the tears covering her cheeks. "But why now?"

"Kayce invited me to her house for Thanksgiving. A group of single people from her church were getting together because none of them had family close by." He turned to Kayce, gazing at her with adoration. "We'd never talked about much besides your soccer, but that day we talked about a lot more." Dad returned his focus to Rainey. "Kayce helped me realize how messed up my life was and asked me to come to church with her the following Sunday. I met the pastor, and we had coffee." He clasped his hands on the table. "I'd pretty much decided it was too late for me. I thought if I could help you achieve your dreams then that would make me a pretty successful father, but I realized that I wanted more for you. You deserve more. You deserved more. I'm so thankful for your grandparents and your mom teaching you about Jesus."

Rainey studied him. "What are you saying?"

"I'm saying I've been baptized, and I'm living with a new purpose. Kayce is part of that, and I hope you'll be, too."

"So you're not pregnant?" Rainey flipped her gaze to Kayce.

"Far from it." Kayce chuckled. "Actually, it'd be impossible. It's true. Your dad is a changed man. I promise I wouldn't be marrying him if he didn't love Jesus as much as I do."

Rainey tucked her chin, shaking her head. Nothing about any of this made sense. Part of her was relieved, but everything inside her was tangled in knots. Was this what she'd wanted from him? It'd been so long; she'd given up years ago on having this kind of father. But he seemed genuine, and Kayce had never given Rainey a reason not to trust her.

"Sweetheart, I love you so much, and I pray that you can forgive me, so we can make a fresh start."

Rainey sighed, lifting her head. "Okay, I forgive you, but I'll need some time to process all of this, especially y'all together."

"We understand. Baby steps." Dad smiled widely.

"Maybe let's table the baby talk. Rainey has enough to consider." Kayce patted Dad's hand.

"I'll get us some menus." Dad crossed the room to the hostess stand.

"Quick, we only have a minute." Kayce leaned in conspiratorially. "What's going on between you and Scott?"

"We're just friends. You know I don't have time to date."

"Rainey, he doesn't act like just a friend. You do realize that?"

"I don't know." She caught her bottom lip between her teeth.

"So he hasn't tried to kiss you?"

"Not recently." Heat burned Rainey's cheeks, but maybe Kayce could help. "When we were in middle school, he tried to on a dare, and well…it didn't end well. Actually, it's kind of haunted me."

"And this all happened around the time your dad left. I can see how it all combined to make you avoid romance."

"I mean, maybe." And it did make sense. Did she want to kiss Scott? He'd seemed ready to kiss her at the batting cage. Her heart squeezed at the thought of being in his arms, and then her heart flipped before it nosedived into her stomach. It was impossible on so many levels. Rainey wrung the napkin. "It doesn't matter. I can't get involved with Scott romantically. It would ruin our friendship, and besides, I don't need the distraction."

"Maybe it's exactly what you need." Kayce arched her brows. "Have some fun, fall in love, live in the moment. I've been telling you for years, the biggest problem with your game is that you don't take risks. You play afraid."

"I don't know how kissing Scott will help, especially when I don't know what I'm doing." She smoothed the napkin on the table, pressing on a wrinkle.

"Rainey, relax." Kayce covered Rainey's hands. "You don't have to kiss him or even date him, but don't avoid romance because you're afraid you won't be perfect."

"I hear you, and I'll try." What would happen if she relaxed and risked her heart?

Chapter Eight

The gentle sea breeze whiffed through Scott's hair as he took his seat for the wedding ceremony. Less than twenty chairs were arranged on either side of a short aisle leading to a simple white arch. The rippling ocean drifted in on low waves that broke with merely a whisper and crept back to the depths with little urgency. As the sun set to the west, strips of fiery colors settled in the sky.

Scott inhaled a deep breath of salty air as peace washed through him, calming his nerves. He hadn't seen Rainey all day. She'd been busy preparing for the ceremony with Kayce and had only texted once to be sure he knew the plans and to tell him to put his meals on her dad's account.

The night before when he'd returned to the restaurant, the trio had been smiling with what seemed like authentic joy, and the conversation had continued easily like they were all old friends. While they'd strolled to their rooms, Rainey told him that her dad had apologized and seemed to be genuinely trying to change his life and his relationship with her. He'd wanted to talk with her more and make sure she was coping well, but after the emotional evening and late dinner, she'd only wanted to go to her room. Giving her space to process alone didn't come naturally to him, but Rainey needed it, and he wanted her to be happy.

Now, a graceful melody blended with the ocean sounds, quieting the chatter of the small congregation. John and his preacher joined the violinist, who'd taken her place beside the arch.

Scott shifted his gaze to the dunes. Rainey appeared first, followed by Kayce and her father. As Rainey crossed the sand, her long blond hair glistened in the rays of the sun, rippling in the wind like the fronds of the palm trees dotting the lawn. Scott's breath caught and his heart tossed. *Radiant.*

Rainey's long pale blue skirt floated around her, while the fitted off-white sweater accented her small waist. When she stopped and regarded him, her eyes were full of peace, almost iridescent blue-gray, like the inside of an oyster shell. When she switched her focus to Kayce, Rainey's lips trembled as Kayce's father gave John her hand.

Following the brief ceremony, the small group moved inside to a second-floor room with picture windows. Rainey posed with Kayce for a photo before finally joining Scott to take in the view of the sunset over the ocean.

"Long time no see." Rainey playfully bumped into his side.

"You're beautiful." His fingers twitched, eager to tuck a lock of loose hair over her ear, but instead he shoved his hands in his pockets. "The view's amazing."

"It is. Maybe later we can go for our walk." She clutched his arm and tugged him away from the windows. "But first let's check out the buffet. I'm starving."

"I doubt there's anything up to your nutritional standards."

"I'm not even a little concerned. We're going to eat all the salty yummy food and wedding cake until we can't eat anymore." Laughing, she patted her belly.

"You're very not Rainey-like tonight."

"It's my dad's wedding, and I'm actually happy for him and Kayce. And I feel like letting loose, having fun, living in the moment without worrying about all the consequences." She spun in front of him and hooked his arm. "Are you in?"

"I think I better keep a close eye on you, party girl."

"Yes." Rainey punched a fist in the air. "We're going to have the best time." Giggling, she headed to the table filled with food. On a large plate, she piled fried shrimp, crabcakes and hush puppies over a mound of cheese grits.

After they finished eating dinner, Kayce's dad toasted the couple, and they cut the wedding cake.

While Rainey talked with some of the members of Kayce and John's life group, Scott got them two pieces of cake. When Rainey said she planned to let loose, Scott hadn't really believed she'd follow through, but after she cleared her plate and went back for seconds, he didn't know what to expect. Now, she chatted easily with virtual strangers, laughing even. Maybe she did just need a day off, and she certainly deserved it.

As the couple finished their conversation with Rainey, Scott passed her the plate with a large slice of cake. "Is this piece big enough for the party girl?"

"I doubt I'll be able to eat more than half." She led them to their seats. "Apparently, my stomach isn't quite as large as my imagination, but I have to taste this cake." She sliced a bite, making sure to get all the layers and a generous portion of the icing. "Kayce said it's lemon elderflower cake with lemon curd, and the icing is elderflower Swiss buttercream." Rainey slid the cake into her mouth, and her eyes nearly rolled back into her head.

"So it's good?" Laughing, Scott scooped a large piece onto his tongue, and the tart lemon flavor balanced with something floral as the salty buttercream melted into the cake. Maybe he could convince Rainey to learn how to bake one of these.

"I wish I could eat it all," she said before delighting in another taste.

He approached her plate with his fork. "I'm happy to help you out."

Giggling, Rainey slid it out of his reach. "I'm not ready to give up yet." But after a few more bites, she groaned. "You win."

He lowered his fork to his plate. "Actually, I've reached my limit, too."

Reclining in her chair, Rainey placed her palms on her stomach. "Do you know I've barely been on a vacation in ten years, and I think the last piece of cake that I ate was on my sixteenth birthday."

"Are you serious?"

"As a red card." She tilted her head, studying him, and as he held her gaze, her small smile morphed into a wide one. "Race you to the beach." She popped out of her seat and lifted her skirt to her ankles, revealing light blue Converse. "Kayce knows me so well." Dropping her skirt, she pivoted for the door.

"Don't you want to grab a jacket? It might be cold." Lunging after her, Scott caught her wrist.

"I'll be fine. This sweater is an angora-and-merino wool blend." She nabbed his hand and slid his palm over the arm. "It's like wearing a sheep."

At her contact, a wave of warmth rushed through him, ensuring he wouldn't need any extra layers, either. In fact, he probably needed to get outside and cool off before he gave in to his persuasive heart and took her in his arms and—

Scott slipped out of her grasp. Why did she have to be so great? "Let's at least tell John and Kayce where we're going." He strode across the room, heat creeping over his skin.

Rainey stopped at his side, her knuckles grazing his. "Dad, Scott and I are going for a quick walk on the beach."

"Sounds nice." Kayce stared off dreamily.

"I do need to talk to you before you leave. Let's meet for breakfast about seven thirty. Will that work?" Dad asked.

"Sure." Rainey's fingers slid around Scott's. "Congratulations. See you in the morning."

"Congrat—" His voice screeched, and he cleared his throat, but his whole face burned. "Congratulations."

"Thank you. Y'all, don't stay out too late." John straightened, squaring his shoulders. "Nothing good happens in the dark."

"Okay." Rainey grimaced.

But Scott met John's stern expression with what he hoped was assurance. "Yes, sir."

"Good night." Rainey pulled Scott out of the room. At the top of the stairs, she stopped and tightened her grip. "I think I like holding your hand." Tilting her head, she met his gaze. "Is that okay?" She whispered almost too quietly for him to hear, but his heart understood and pounded like it would explode. Was this just her innocence and inexperience or did she want more?

Staring into her eyes, he searched for the answer. They softened to a quiet blue-gray as a blush highlighted her cheeks, but the clues her expression gave weren't conclusive given her past. He'd have to let her lead the way and hope he could figure out where she was going. Scott squeezed her hand. "I like holding your hand, too. Ready for our walk?"

Without answering or letting go, Rainey started down the stairs. As they exited the building, the roar of the ocean greeted them.

"I guess the tide changed." Rainey guided them through the dunes. "I've never done this."

"What do you mean? You said y'all came to the beach in elementary school."

"But not at night and not with a boy." She swung their hands as they proceeded over the sand.

"I'm not exactly a boy."

"Trust me, I'm very aware of that distinction."

"I'm glad because I'm a very different boy than the one you met in middle school, and I hope you know that you can trust me. I really want you to be happy." The fine sea mist cooled his skin, tempering his adrenaline.

"I absolutely never imagined that we would be on a moon-lit beach stroll when I was eleven, but I do trust you. You've been such a good friend the last couple of weeks. I know I can be difficult—always seeking perfection. Kayce says it keeps me from playing my best." As they continued to move against the wind, Rainey's hair waved behind them.

"I'll defer to your coach for soccer, but as far as I'm concerned, you've been anything but difficult. I've asked a lot of you, and you've jumped right in. Since you got to town, my life hasn't seemed so lonely."

"Same. I like spending time with you." Rainey stopped and shifted in front of him, finding his other hand. "I'm sorry if I was distant after the batting lesson." She inclined her face, rolling her lips as she looked into his eyes.

"No, that was my fault. I overstepped." And he was about to again, as he got lost in her gaze, but she was moving closer.

"You didn't overstep. I got scared because of everything before, you know, but I don't think I am anymore." She moved her hands up his arms to his shoulders as she closed the distance between them.

"I'm so sorry for all of that. I would never want you to be afraid."

"I'm not. I actually feel safe with you."

"I'm glad." He rested his palms on her back, lowering his lips to meet hers.

But a breath before her lips made contact with his, she ducked her chin, landing her forehead against his chest. "Sorry."

Scott exhaled, resting his cheek on her head. "Rainey, do you want to kiss me?"

"Yes, but—"

"No *buts*. I want to kiss you, too." Scott slipped his hand under her chin.

"I've never—"

"I know."

"I don't want to mess it up." She pressed her lips together, her breaths shallow against his body.

"I don't think that's possible." He smiled, delight seeping through him. "Would it help if I kissed you?"

"If you don't mind."

"Not at all." Scott slid his fingers to the base of her head as he lowered his lips to hers, melding them together slowly, calming her quivering mouth with his. Rainey's eyelids feathered closed as she yielded to his leading. With a tenderness and patience he didn't know he possessed, he shut his own eyes and savored the moment. Never had a kiss met him on this level.

Bliss bubbled in Rainey's belly as Scott kissed her. She clung to him, never wanting this moment to end. Her lips tingled with the sensation of his warm mouth on hers, accepting her for who she was and not asking for more. She loved being in his arms, not worrying about anything because he was taking care of her. He wanted her to be happy, and he wouldn't let her fail, at least not at kissing, but she was pretty sure he'd do everything in his power to help her succeed at whatever she wanted.

"Rainey," Scott whispered against her face, sending a pleasant round of shivers down her shoulders. "You are perfection." He hugged her close, wrapping his arms completely around her and kissing the top of her head. "I hope I didn't disappoint you."

"Not a chance. This has been the best night." Resting her cheek on his chest, she tickled the little curls at the nape of his neck. "Can we stay here a little longer? Maybe you could give me one more lesson before we leave."

He chuckled. "I'm happy to kiss you more, but you don't need any lessons."

"I'm starting to realize how much I have to learn. Besides cooking healthy and soccer, I'm a novice at everything."

"Maybe that's not all bad." Scott brushed a lock of hair from her face, curling it around his finger. "Some of my experiences I wish hadn't happened."

"Like with women?"

"Definitely."

Definitely. Her ribs constricted. How many women had he dated?

"Rainey, my past love life isn't that bad. You can relax."

"What? I'm relaxed." She rolled her shoulders, trying to release the tension.

"Nice try."

"I don't even have enough experience to guess how bad your *love* life could've been. This is so embarrassing." Lifting her head, she pressed away from him.

"Whoa. Where do you think you're going?" He caught the back of her head and brought their foreheads together. "May I have a moment to explain before you dash away?"

"Okay. I guess."

"First of all, *love* life is just an expression." He peered at her like he was making sure she was listening.

"So you haven't been in love?"

"Wow." He shifted his attention to the sky. "You get right to the point, don't you?"

She fidgeted with his lapel. "You don't have to answer."

"It's not that. I just need a second. Less than twenty-four hours ago, we were just friends, and now we're kissing and sharing rather intimate details of our lives." Scott returned his focus to her, but also loosened his embrace, creating space between them. Space she didn't want and didn't understand. Why did she always ask the wrong question?

"I assure you if you were about to tell me anything intimate, I do not want to hear it." She covered her ears. "We can just be friends if that's what you want."

He clasped her wrist and moved her hands from her ears. "That is not what I want. I know you love efficiency, but we can't have an entire relationship in one day." His hands fell onto that lovely spot on her back, holding her safely. "We're just getting started, and yes, I have dated a few women. Most of those relationships have been pretty forgettable."

"I like forgettable."

"Me, too, but I don't want you imagining anything else, so I'm not through."

"Okay."

"Before the accident, I'd been in an on-again, off-again relationship for about two years, and we both finally seemed to be on the same page and ready to commit to something more long-lasting." His chest rose beneath her palms as he inhaled a slow, deep breath. "I don't know if we were really *in love*, but we did care a lot about each other, or at least I thought we did. Anyway, when I told Dawn that I was quitting baseball and moving home to take care of Henry, she acted like it would be okay, but after a couple of weekends with Henry and Champ and my parents and the rest of Woodley, she bolted with barely a goodbye."

"That's terrible, but honestly, maybe you dodged a bullet."

"Still, it's a lot to ask of anyone to join me in this chaos. Half the time I want to run away myself."

"But you don't because you're a good man." She placed her palms against the bristles on his jaw. "You are doing a great job with everything thrown at you."

"It's hard not to compare myself to Hank. I don't think I'll ever be as good at this life as him."

"You need to give yourself time. It hasn't even been a year. Sure, you won't be as good as Hank at being Hank, but you are a great Scott, so be him. I for one think he's a pretty terrific guy." She brushed her thumbs over the short whiskers at the corners of his lips. "And for what it's worth, he's a really good kisser."

"So now you're an expert." He drew her to him, their noses nearly touching.

"I had the best coach." She slid her hands around his head and pressed her lips to his, delighting in him and exploring this life without fear.

Chapter Nine

Sipping his coffee, Scott averted his eyes from the bright rays of the sun rising over the ocean. With more concentration than seemed necessary, Rainey stirred granola and dried berries into her Greek yogurt. She'd barely uttered a word since she'd stepped out of her room and walked with him to the hotel restaurant. The hostess had suggested the table by the large easterly facing window so they could enjoy the sunrise, and it'd served as a nice distraction from Rainey's silent treatment—a complete one-eighty from her playful attitude the night before. Even more than cold, she seemed distant, gone to a place she didn't intend to invite him.

"Good morning." Gazing out the window, John gripped the back of a chair. "Isn't it beautiful here? Hard to believe people don't believe in God with that kind of majesty on display." He kissed Rainey's head and sat.

"Morning." Rainey spared her dad a smile, continuing to stir her breakfast concoction.

"Thank you for meeting me. I didn't want to wake Kayce, but please know how much you being with us meant to her and how proud she is of you."

"When y'all get home from the cruise, I plan to come for a long visit if I'm not training with a club."

"As much as we'd love to have you, we hope this tryout will be the one." John beamed almost as brightly as the sun.

Rainey dropped her spoon, catapulting a glob of yogurt and granola onto the table. "Dad, what are you saying? Do I have a tryout scheduled?"

"I got the call Friday afternoon, but we had so much going on with the wedding, it seemed like a good idea to wait to discuss it with you."

"Oh, wow. This is amazing." Rainey pressed a shaky hand to her cheek. "Thanks, Dad."

Scott's chest tightened. He wanted to be happy for her. He couldn't hold her back. What they'd shared had been nice, but it was just a couple of kisses. Amazing kisses, but nonetheless, this was her dream, and he needed to say something. He forced a smile that he hoped appeared encouraging. "Congratulations."

Rainey's attention jerked to him like she'd forgotten he was at the table. "Thanks." Holding his gaze, she touched her lips but then dropped her hand to the table as she faced her dad. It was finished. Whatever had developed between them had just ended without a single word.

As resignation settled inside Scott, the biscuit covered in sausage gravy that had seemed so delicious now turned his stomach, but he didn't trust his face not to reveal his true feelings, so he continued to regard the pieces of sausage drowning in the thick, white mixture.

"You have two more weeks to train, but don't overdo it. We don't want you injured. You'll join the team for training the first two weeks of March in Orlando."

"I'll be ready. I've been feeling really healthy."

"What about your hamstring?" John asked.

While Scott had seen Rainey use the roller on her legs, it'd seemed like part of her routine, but apparently her injury was worse than she'd let on. What else did he not know about her? Sure, they'd shared a lot, but clearly not everything. When he chanced a glance, John and Rainey were focused entirely on each other, so Scott slumped back, crossing his arms over his stomach. He probably could have left without their notice.

"It's great. I've been doing lots of stretches and strength training." She filled her spoon. "Nothing to worry about. I won't disappoint you."

"Honey, you could never disappoint me." John folded his hands on the table, studying Rainey. "I know we've never discussed other paths for you, and I don't want you to think I don't believe in you, but if this doesn't work out or you change your mind about a pro career and decide to retire, it'll be okay. There's more to life than soccer. And just to be clear, I'm not saying you should retire, but God may have something else for you. Who would have thought your soccer would be what brought me to know Him and fall in love with Kayce? God works in ways that we don't always understand."

"But I believe this is the path God has chosen for me. It has to be." With her napkin, Rainey swiped the yogurt off the table.

"I hope so, and Kayce and I will be praying for you."

"Thanks, Dad. Please thank Kayce for me." Rainey nodded, her jaw set and shoulders squared.

Scott knew that stance. He'd seen it in the mirror. Determination at all costs. Nothing would stand in her way, certainly not a man and a little boy living in a small town. His stomach hollowed with lost hope, but he did want this happiness for Rainey. With equal resolve, he'd hide his pain behind a smile.

"I will. And speaking of my darling wife, I'm going to go get her breakfast from the Cottage Coffee Shop." John stood. "Y'all have a safe trip. I'll have Kayce call you before we board the ship to discuss anything you might want to focus on for the tryout." His gaze fell to Rainey, and his expression softened with so much love and pride. "Rainey, I love you no matter what."

Rainey rose and hugged her dad. "I love you."

At least their relationship had been restored. When John released Rainey, Scott stood and extended his hand. "It was great to meet you, sir."

"You, too." John shook Scott's hand. "I hope we'll be seeing more of you."

Scott's chest tensed, but he maintained his expression. What could he say? He couldn't affirm the man's statement. The words wouldn't come. Instead, he said, "Have a nice vacation."

"Thanks." With a smile that lit up his eyes, John almost skipped from the restaurant.

"You've hardly touched your breakfast." Rainey pointed her spoon at Scott's plate. Somehow during the conversation, she'd eaten half of her yogurt mixture.

"I think I'm still full from last night." A whirlpool of emotions churned in his stomach. There was no way he could eat. Scott dropped his napkin over his plate. "Ready to go?"

"Yes, if we leave now, I should be able to get in a full workout before supper." She hopped up from the table. Apparently, Rainey didn't want to dwell on whatever *they* were, and he didn't need to wallow in it, either. She would go to her tryout, and he would return to his life. Everything would simply be the way it was before she'd invaded his days. It would be fine.

As she jogged by the grove of olive trees, Rainey pulled off her long-sleeved top and tied it about her waist as she started the trek back to town. Now was not the time to quit. With a burst of adrenaline, she sprinted for the high school.

Of course, playing soccer was what God wanted. Why

else would He have given her this talent and all this success? Having Dad actually care about her well-being was nice, but not at the expense of him giving up on her dreams. The goals they'd focused on for more than fifteen years. And what did he mean telling Scott he'd hoped to see him again? Did he really think she'd let a man distract her when she was this close to realizing everything she'd ever wanted?

Everything she'd ever wanted. The words jumbled in her brain, and the memory of Scott's tender touch and sweet words swirled around her heart. She'd been completely out of control, overcome with the romance of the wedding and the beach, not to mention the sugar overload. It didn't matter the cause or the result. Her priority must be preparing for the tryout. She'd have two weeks of training with the team to prove herself worthy of a spot, or she'd be boarding a plane for Iceland or Australia for one of the summer leagues.

Surely, Scott understood. They hadn't talked much on the ride from the beach. She didn't know what to say. Her lips still tingled from the kisses, and even though he said she wasn't bad at it, he'd likely just been being kind. How desperate must she have appeared? Every time she dared a peek at him, the ripples in her stomach swelled to waves of nausea. Could they even go back to just being friends? It didn't matter. She didn't have time to indulge in distractions.

At the front of the high school, where she'd left her gear, Rainey collapsed over her thighs, an intense pain slicing through her hamstring. She inhaled sharply, holding the breath and willing the oxygen to her strained muscle. It would only take a few more minutes and some deep breaths and then the muscles would relax. If only the same exercises would work on her heart.

Life had been so much simpler when it'd only been her

and soccer. She just needed to return to that place. Her team-mates, coaches and trainers were her family.

Rainey grabbed her water bottle from the ground, then she rolled her spine straight. She took a swig, tossed her bag over her shoulder and trekked to the baseball field. With her leg muscles warm, she could practice her shooting. She'd do her ab workout later—

Rainey stopped at the gate, her pulse kicking up to a sprint.

Scott stood in the soccer goal, and Henry dribbled around three orange cones and kicked the ball. It rolled by Scott, who pretended to try and stop it. "Great shot."

Taking a step backward, Rainey scanned the area for a place to hide. She needed more time to box up her feelings before she faced—

"Rainey." Henry dashed across the field.

"Hi." She waved as she opened the gate. "Did you have fun with your grandparents?"

"Yes, but I missed you." With his little arms, he hugged away her resolve. "Did you see my goal?"

"It was great. I can tell you've been practicing." She could do this. They could be friends, and she could still train, and the warmth embracing her heart was only because Scott was being so sweet to Henry.

"Hey, we can leave." Scott tossed Henry's ball between his palms. "I know you need to train, and I told Henry if you came, we'd have to go."

"You don't have to leave. I mean, I can always use some-one to grab the balls that I overshoot." Rainey crouched in front of Henry. "Can you be my ball boy?"

"Yes."

"That's not necessary. Henry, let's give Rainey the field. She doesn't need us in the way."

"I said it's fine." Rainey rose, challenging his glare. So much for Scott being sweet.

"Please, Uncle Scott, please."

She gave him a one-shoulder shrug, smirking.

"It's fine, but only because Rainey asked you." With his eyes fixed on hers, he raised both his eyebrows.

Rainey snatched her focus away but not in time to stop the wave of felicity swelling within her. Maybe they were back where they'd started, and maybe it would be okay… Maybe.

She ripped open her bag and dumped the balls on the grass. "Do you mind?" She dribbled the ball in front of him.

"Yes, ma'am," he said with one of his lopsided grins before jogging behind the goal. "Come on, Henry. I'll help you."

Rainey planted her left foot and kicked the ball with her right, sending it toward the goal. It hit the crossbar and went wide, and Henry ran after it. Rainey grimaced as she hooked another ball with her toe, waiting to hear Scott's snide remark, but he said nothing.

She took a deep breath and rolled her shoulders. If nothing else, this kind of training would be good for her concentration. She kicked the ball into the net and a rush of satisfaction eased through her, loosening her tight muscles.

After she'd filled the net with balls, missing only enough to keep Henry entertained, she called a water break. At some point during the session, the awkward tension had waned. Hopefully, it'd stay away.

While Henry packed the balls into Rainey's bag, Scott jogged over. "Thanks for letting us hang out. It meant a lot to Henry."

"Did you tell him about my tryout?" She gulped from the bottle.

"I thought you'd like to."

"Okay. I'm sorry that I'm leaving you to coach the soccer clinic."

"Hey, you know I'm happy for you, and Henry will be, too." He nudged her side. "We always knew your time here was temporary. This is an amazing opportunity, and you shouldn't worry about us. We'll be fine. We want you to have your dream."

"Thanks." Rainey twisted the top on her bottle. Sweet Scott had made a return, and he was making her insides all squishy, but at the same time, he was giving her the space and encouragement she needed. He was a really good friend. Maybe another time, they could have more, but for now, she'd be thankful for his friendship.

"Henry, come here. Rainey has something exciting to tell you." Scott patted her shoulder. "You've got this."

Chapter Ten

Monday evening, Scott dropped the stack of paperwork on the dining-room table and collapsed into a chair. Who knew being a PE teacher would require so much homework? For over a week, he'd hidden in the busyness of his routine, trying not to notice the days going by, staying preoccupied because he really wasn't sure if he wanted to slow down time or speed it up. Right now, he just wanted a break from it all.

After a long practice with the varsity baseball team, he'd picked up Henry from his parents' and come home only to have Champ barrel out of the kitchen and under the backyard fence. He'd been meaning to find a solution that would keep Champ from chasing the squirrels, but he hadn't had a free minute. When he'd left to chase the dog, he'd told Henry to put away the groceries. But when he returned, the groceries were still on the kitchen table, and Henry was on the couch, playing *FIFA World Cup.*

After Scott put away the groceries, he'd brought in the work he needed to complete. But here he sat, hungry, tired and completely unmotivated. He could order a pizza, or they could eat cold cereal. A few weeks ago, cereal had seemed fine, but Rainey's constant speeches on nutrition had transformed Henry into a health nut. The kid knew more about vitamins, protein and healthy grains than he did about superheroes.

Scott slammed his palms on the table. "Henry, please get a bath, while I make supper."

"Five more minutes." Like he could tell time. In the beginning, Scott had given into this trick. Until he realized that Henry always said it to buy time, while Scott got distracted.

But Henry wasn't the only one learning new skills. Scott stalked into the living room. "Now."

"But I'm about to win the World Cup."

"You can win the World Cup tomorrow." Scott took the controller from Henry. "Bath."

"You're so mean." Henry stormed down the hall and slammed the bathroom door.

Scott winced, a pang of guilt striking at his resolve. He should reprimand Henry, but they were finally connecting, and he didn't let him get away with nearly as much as he used to. Hadn't he read on some parenting blog that it was okay to pick your battles?

After a supper of chicken tacos made with whole-wheat tortillas and topped with enough veggies to please Henry, they each savored one of Rainey's chocolate banana peanut-butter treats. Once Henry brushed his teeth and settled on the couch, Scott found a soccer game for the boy to watch.

But Scott slumped in front of his work. Why had he taken on the fundraiser?

Henry. It all came down to Henry's happiness, and it made all the sleepless nights worth it. With Rainey leaving, he'd need to delegate her responsibilities. But first, he needed to register for the exams required to complete his teacher's certification. With his college degree, he'd been able to take over Hank's job on a provisional certificate, but if he wanted to keep it, this needed to be his first priority. Scott signed into the site. After he registered, he'd enter the grades for the nine-week rotation. They still had a week left before grades were due, but he had a baseball tournament to win.

When would he have time to figure out how to coach soccer? He raked his fingers through his hair. Even if it was only a couple hours a week, it took time. Maybe once Rainey was gone, Henry would let it go, but how would Henry react when she left? He'd seemed excited about her tryout, but he didn't understand that she wouldn't be around at all.

How had a week already gone by since they'd returned from the wedding? Each day he considered forcing Henry and himself to face the reality that their time with Rainey was ending, but he kept putting it off.

The weight of it all pressed against Scott's shoulders, but he rolled them back and tossed off the blues. Maybe Henry could be a batboy for the team. He could order him a uniform, and after school let out for summer vacation, they could drive to Atlanta and catch some Braves games. As he completed the forms, he built a wall around his heart. It wasn't the life he'd planned, but he needed to be strong for Henry, and he could find joy in Henry's happiness, in the baseball team's victories, and maybe one day, he'd fall in love—

The doorbell chimed, yanking him from his thoughts. He checked the form on the screen and hit Submit. One thing off his seemingly endless list. "Henry, it's about time for bed." He opened the front door.

Rainey dangled a whistle over a binder and a couple of books. "Sorry it's late, but I got stuck on a video call with one of my former teammates helping her make dinner for her fiancé."

"It's fine." He made room for her to enter. "What's all this?"

"Everything you need to coach soccer—a rule book, a book on coaching young players, my personal binder of drills, a picture book for Henry and a whistle because all coaches need a whistle. Right? You probably already have one, but I couldn't resist."

"Thanks." Forcing a smile, he took the items. *Great*. Just what he needed, more homework.

Henry patted the spot next to him on the couch. "Rainey, come watch the game."

"Hey, buddy, I can't stay. I have to get to bed." She checked her watch. "To be a great soccer player, you have to get a good night's sleep."

"Oh." Henry narrowed his eyes, studying her. He was pretty intuitive when it came to the psychological tricks adults used to persuade kids. If he went to bed, it would be to please Rainey, not because it would make him a better soccer player. But maybe Scott could give the little guy the motivation to help him make his decision.

"Rainey brought you a book." He held up the picture book with the dinosaur kicking a soccer ball on the cover. "We could read it tonight if you go to bed now."

"Could Rainey read it to me?" Henry looked between the two adults.

"Do you have time?"

"Sure. Let's go."

"Do you mind if I keep working?" Scott gestured at the table blanketed with papers, notebooks, a binder and his glowing laptop. "I'm swamped."

"No problem." Concern creased her forehead. "I'm sorry—"

He held up his hand. "Don't apologize."

"Okay. We'll be quiet."

"Come on, Rainey." Henry tugged on her.

"Yes, sir." Rainey let the little boy guide her from the room.

As they rounded the corner, their voices became hushed. Rainey probably told Henry to whisper.

Scott's heart pressed against the wall he'd just constructed. How could this seem so perfect and completely wrong all at the same time? He needed to keep his distance, put more space between them all. At least tomorrow would be the last soccer clinic with her, and he had the out-of-town baseball tournament. Then again, maybe he should be spending as much time with her as possible, but that wouldn't be best for Henry.

Scott stalked to the table and logged in to the grade portal. At least he'd have plenty to keep busy. He finished entering the grades and sent two texts to the group chat, scheduling a fundraiser committee meeting, and was finally able to concentrate on making the last arrangements for Rainey's surprise party, when she tapped his shoulder, startling him. He flipped over his notebook. Hopefully, she hadn't seen his checklist.

"Sorry." She retreated, braiding her fingers. "I think he's asleep, so I'm going."

"Thanks." His nerves twitched to reach for her hands, to keep her here, to simply touch her, but he clenched his hands under the table. *Let her go. Be her friend. Let her be happy.*

Misinterpreting or maybe correctly interpreting his reaction, Rainey retreated to the door. "See you later."

"Yep." He turned to his screen as the door clicked shut. Less than a week of this torture left. Why had he agreed to surprise her with a sendoff celebration?

After Scott's indifference to her dropping by, Rainey didn't know where they stood. Although had she ever really known? She arranged two small goal nets and used cones to create a boundary. For her last training session, they were going to play a game—boys versus girls. Henry had pouted when she'd told him her idea, but she wanted him to see his uncle as his new coach. She'd make sure they ended on time, so Scott's baseball practice wasn't delayed. They were headed to a tournament, and the guy needed a win.

Once the kids warmed up, Rainey helped the girls put on pink pinnies, while Scott aided his teammates with blue ones.

"A little help." With the pinny over one arm and his head, Scott contorted, trying to get his other arm through the hole.

"Be still." Rainey shifted the opening over his arm and jerked the material over his muscular chest. "All set." She gave his pecs a pat, instantly regretting the action as heat skipped over her skin. "Okay, so, um, everyone get in the starting formation. Guys, y'all kick off first." She placed the ball in the center of the makeshift field.

Henry raised his hand. "What about the goalie?"

"Since we're playing three versus three, we won't have one, and also—" she smirked "—no throw-ins."

"What?" Scott smacked his thighs.

"The field's too small."

"Exactly. I could pitch it into the goal from the sideline." He mimicked throwing the ball over his head like she'd taught the kids.

"Kind of goes against the spirit of the game. Don't you think?"

"You and I both know that you care as much about winning as I do."

"Too bad. I'm still the coach, and I make the rules." She blew her whistle. "Liam, pass the ball to Henry or Coach Scott."

Liam followed directions, sending the ball to Scott. But Mindy sprinted between them, stole the ball and dribbled into the goal before anyone else could react. The girl was a natural with a mind for the game. She'd go far if soccer could ever get off the ground in Woodley.

A pang of guilt pricked Rainey's resolve, but she shoved it away, joining Emma and Mindy in a group hug. "Way to go, Mindy!"

As the girls returned to their positions, Henry retrieved the ball and put it on the center line. "Uncle Scott, you have to go to the ball."

"Dude, she came out of nowhere."

"Whatever." Henry kicked the ball to Liam, and they made a nice run at their goal, slipping by Emma before Mindy intercepted the ball on the goal line. But Scott ran interference on their next attempt, and the boys scored. Still, at the end of the game, the girls won.

"It really wasn't fair between you being a pro and Mindy's being a protégé." Scott shook Rainey's hand. "Next time, I'm choosing the teams."

"We'll see." Rainey gripped his hand tighter. "I'm going to miss this." She sniffled, blinking away unexpected tears.

"Hey, none of that." Scott pulled her into a hug. "Kids, are you ready?"

"Yes."

Scott turned her around slowly.

"Surprise!" the children shouted, tossing confetti. "Congratulations!"

"Wh-what's all this?" Rainey stammered.

Henry clasped her hand. "An ice-cream-sundae party!"

"But Scott, what about baseball practice?"

"I canceled it." He squeezed her shoulders. "One night off isn't going to hurt."

"Right this way." Mindy guided Rainey to the side of the field, where the moms had set up a table with ice cream and assorted toppings.

"Wow. Thank you."

"Henry wanted to do something special for your last practice, so I got the other parents to help me put this together."

"Well, now I kind of feel bad about beating you."

"No, you don't."

"You're right, I don't." She took a bowl of ice cream from Mindy's mom. "This is really sweet of y'all."

"It's the least we could do. We're all so excited for you," she said.

Liam's mom scooped ice cream in the kids' bowls. "From what Scott's said, the tryout sounds like an amazing opportunity. I know he and Henry will miss you."

"We all will. The travel must make it hard on relationships. Do your parents make it to any of your games? I can't imagine missing one of Mindy's events." Mindy's mom hugged the girl to her side.

"Well, I've played overseas mostly, so it's not really convenient, but Orlando is only a couple of hours from Jacksonville, so maybe Dad will make the home games." While several professional players had families, Rainey would never be an absentee parent like Dad had been. It'd nearly ruined their relationship, but it wasn't like it mattered. She didn't have a kid.

Distracted. Every player had lacked focus and determination, and it'd cost them the tournament. As the bus rolled into the high-school parking lot, Scott fixed his jaw. What did he expect from the team when their coach was preoccupied with soccer, not to mention Rainey?

The loss ended and started with him. Hank would never have allowed this to happen. He took this team to State only a year ago. Of all the things Scott thought he'd fail doing, coaching his brother's team hadn't been one of them. He knew baseball, and he knew how to win. His square-dance lessons may have ended in a lot of squished toes, and Henry may have eaten too much cold cereal and played too many video games, but winning baseball games is what he did, and he wouldn't let Hank or these boys down again.

Henry's happiness was his priority, and thankfully, he seemed to be happy, but how long could Scott count on that once Rainey left, and soccer had to take a back seat to baseball? How did Hank do this? For one thing, there wasn't a soccer goal in his outfield, and soon there wouldn't be one in Scott's.

Frustration clamped the base of his skull as the bus came to a stop. Scott stood in the aisle. "Take the rest of the weekend to kill any distractions. Beginning Monday, we're focused on winning. We have the entire season in front of us. This tournament was a wake-up call. I expect everyone to give practices and games your full attention. Understood?"

"Yes, Coach," the team mumbled.

"Let's try that again. Understood?"

"Yes, Coach," they said, their voices rising.

"No distractions." Scott punched his fist in the air.

"No distractions," the team responded.

Scott jogged down the bus steps, tossed his duffel in the jeep and continued to the field. *No distractions.* The soccer goal had to go. He'd planned to wait until Rainey left to remove it, but what was one day?

When he rounded the field house, a ball smashed into the fence. Apparently, he was one day too soon.

"Didn't expect to see you today." Rainey stood behind a row of balls.

"Just got back from the tournament and thought I'd do some work before heading home."

She dribbled toward him. "How'd it go?"

"Not great." And things weren't improving.

"Losing is never fun." With her toe, Rainey flipped the ball in the air and bounced it on her knee. "Where's Henry?" She juggled the ball to her other knee and back before sending it to her hands.

"He's at home with his new sitter, Sue." Tension radiated from the base of his skull.

"Oh, I thought he stayed with your parents. I could have spent the night with him."

"Rainey, you're leaving tomorrow afternoon." He pressed his fingers between his eyebrows "We have to figure things out for the long term. I'm going to need a lot more help during baseball season."

"Right. I hope y'all have a winning season. I'm sorry I won't be here to cheer you on."

"It's fine." He rubbed the stubble on his chin. "How much longer do you think you'll be out here? I want to get that goal moved."

"What about the clinic and Henry's team?"

"We're going to have to put the clinic on hold until we have more help."

"But—"

"Rainey, look, I'm grateful for all you've done for Henry, but I need my team focused on baseball. This is a major distraction...for them."

She raised her brow. "Are you seriously blaming that net for your loss?"

"It certainly didn't help." Why was she questioning him? He just wanted to do what was best for the team, and it wasn't like he meant to interfere with her practice. Why couldn't she just tell him when she'd be through? He swallowed, trying to gain some composure. "All I asked was when you'd be finished, so I could deal with it. I don't want to do anything to compromise your tryout, but you're not the only one with a career to consider." Those were not the words he meant to say. He ground his molars.

"Wow." She held up a hand. "I knew you were bitter about losing your pro career, but I thought our friendship was beyond jealousy."

"I'm not bitter, and I'm not jealous." Was he? No, he wanted her to be successful and happy.

"You sure about that?" She dropped the ball to her feet. "Don't bother answering. You can't be honest with me because you haven't been honest with yourself." Turning away from him, she planted her foot and then sent the ball soaring toward the goal. "Do what you want with the goal. I'm through." She charged away.

What had he done? Regret knotted his stomach. He needed to apologize. She was his friend. He wasn't jealous. He was losing…at everything. Scott grabbed the fence and jumped over it. "Rainey, wait. I'm sorry."

His phone buzzed in his pocket, but it could wait. He hurried after her. "I shouldn't have said that." He caught her wrist, halting her. "This loss hit hard. I know I shouldn't but I feel guilty about Hank and Kristen's deaths, and I want to make him proud, but once again, I've failed."

"You aren't failing." Rainey folded her hand around his. "You're learning, and you can't punish yourself every time you mess up. Hank would never want that."

"I guess, but—" His phone vibrated again, and he checked the display and answered. "Hi, Sue, I'll be home—"

"Henry's missing," Sue said.

"What?" Scott gripped the phone.

"Henry's gone. I've searched everywhere. I was in the kitchen making a snack, and when I went out back, he was gone, and so was Champ."

The fence. He dropped Rainey's hand, adrenaline surging through him. "Did you check with Tommy's parents?"

"Yes. I've asked all the neighbors. Everyone is searching, but we can't find him. I called your parents, but they're still on the road."

"Did you check the shed? Under his bed? All the closets? Under the house?"

"Yes." Sue sobbed. "Everywhere. He's not here."

"What's wrong?" Rainey sprinted after him.

"Henry's missing and so is Champ."

"I'll go with you."

When they reached Scott's jeep, they both leaped inside. Scott started the engine, but as he shifted into Reverse, he grimaced and tossed his phone to Rainey. "See who that is."

"It's Sue." She tapped the screen, answering on speaker. "Hi, this is Rainey. I'm with Scott."

"The Merrills just brought Champ home. Somehow—"

"What about Henry?" Scott shouted, white-knuckling the steering wheel as he sped onto the street.

"No sign of him."

"Where did they find Champ?" Rainey scanned the sides of the road, her pulse pounding as she tried to stay calm for Scott.

"Under a picnic table at the park."

"How long has Henry been missing?"

"Between forty-five minutes and an hour. I didn't want to worry you, Scott. I thought I'd find them. I'm sorry."

"Just take Champ inside and stay at the house in case Henry comes home," Rainey said.

"Yes, ma'am." Sue ended the call.

"At least we know where not to search. Where does Champ usually go when he gets out?" Rainey asked.

"Wherever the squirrels run, which is usually farther into the woods behind our house."

"So Henry probably went that way."

"Right. Champ wouldn't cross the creek, and I don't think Henry would, either. At least I hope not." Scott concentrated on the road, while he tugged a cross from under his shirt and clutched it. "I can't believe I lost him."

He turned on the straightaway leading out of town and slammed on the gas.

"Where are you going?" On her runs, she hadn't seen a creek.

"There's a dirt road between the Lindsey farm and one of the Worths' blueberry fields. It ends at the creek. I figure there's a fifty-fifty chance he would go in that direction once he reached the creek." Scott slowed the jeep as they passed the field of green plants and turned at more of a trail than a road. As the jeep bumped over holes and mounds in the road, Scott concentrated on the road, never reducing the speed. "Call Sue. Tell her to have Tom Martin and whoever else search the creek bank and woods going in the other direction."

"Got it." Rainey picked up his phone and made the call as Scott parked at the edge of what Rainey would've called a river, not a creek. *Please, Lord, let Henry be okay.*

Scott jumped from his seat, while she finished giving Sue the directions, and then dashed after him. "Sue's calling Tom now. She said most of the neighbors are out looking," Rainey shouted as Scott ducked into the forest. With the roots and overgrowth, Scott's pace slowed, giving Rainey the chance to nearly catch him. "We'll find him. He'll be okay."

"Henry!" Scott shouted, taking long strides.

Hurrying behind him, she scanned the area. "Henry!"

They surged through the forest, calling his name. After

what felt like hours but was probably only minutes, they heard the boy shouting.

"Champ. Champ." Henry clapped. "Here, boy."

"Henry." Scott nearly tripped before darting through the bushes. "Henry."

Thank God. Relief flooded Rainey as she trekked after Scott, almost losing sight of him as he weaved through the brush, shoving branches out of his way.

As a wiry limb sprung back, nearly smacking her, she caught it and stopped, her heart lifted with a mix of relief, joy and love.

Scott dropped to one knee and gathered Henry, holding him tight. "Thank God, you're okay."

"Uncle Scott?" Henry studied his uncle. "Champ got out. I've been searching everywhere for him. Are you okay? I'm sorry. I should've watched him closer." Henry brushed his fingers under Scott's eyes. "Don't cry Uncle Scott. We'll find him."

"He was at the park, buddy, but he's home now." Holding the boy's face, Scott gazed at his nephew.

"Oh, good." Henry smiled, his focus shifting to Rainey. "Hi, Coach. We finished all the chocolate banana peanut-butter treats. Can you make us some more?"

"I'll try, but if I can't, I'll leave the recipe with my grandma."

"Okay."

"Don't bother Rainey with that. She's leaving for her try-out tomorrow afternoon. Remember?" Scott stood, taking Henry's hand.

"Oh, sorry."

"It's okay, Henry. I'm glad you like them." As they passed her, she ruffled his hair. "I'm so glad we found you. We were so worried." She lowered the wayward branch and followed. "It isn't safe for a little boy to—"

"I've got this," Scott growled. A wrecking ball of regret and rejection split through her, leaving her empty, as if she'd missed the most important goal of her life. But he was right. He needed to be the parent. She was leaving. This wasn't her place. A cool breeze rustled the leaves, chilling Rainey's skin and her emotions. She needed to trust her plans and not be a victim of her feelings. Her future was on the pitch, not in Woodley, Georgia. With slow, steady steps, she followed behind them, keeping her distance.

"Lots of people are worried about you." Scott's shoulders drooped. "I know you care about Champ, but you can't leave the house by yourself. No one knew where you were. Promise me you'll never do something like this again."

"But Champ—"

"No *buts*. We'll take care of Champ together, like we'll take care of each other." Scott slung his arm around Henry. "Got it?"

"Got it."

"Love you, buddy."

"Love you, too, Uncle Scott, and you, too, Rainey," Henry said.

Unable to dislodge the lump in her throat, Rainey gave him the best smile she could muster and patted her chest over her crumbling heart.

When they reached the edge of the woods, Scott clapped Henry on the shoulder. "Go ahead to the jeep. I need to talk to Rainey."

"Okay." Henry skipped across the clearing.

"I'm sorry," Rainey blurted. "I overstepped."

"Don't get me wrong. I appreciate everything you've done for Henry, but we need to start letting go. He needs to deal with the fact that you won't be around. Every time we delay that reality, it makes things more difficult…for Henry."

"I understand."

"So when we drop you off, that's it for tonight. Please don't offer to make supper or dessert or watch one last game. We'll say good-night, and we won't make a big deal out of it."

"Fine."

"Rainey, I know you care about him, but please respect this boundary. It's for the best...for Henry."

"I told you I understand. Let's just go." She climbed into the jeep. This would be better for all of them. Scott was right. Even if it was hard, she'd say goodbye to Henry on a happy note tonight and leave without making a scene. Besides, she didn't need the distraction. She'd put them behind her and focus on what mattered. Her heart pinched, but it was only a pinch, not a reason to change the direction of her life. A professional career was what she'd trained for and what she wanted. Realizing the big dream required sacrifice.

Chapter Eleven

❧

Sunday morning, Henry jumped out of bed and got himself ready for church without any reminders. Maybe Scott had finally gotten through to him, but unease quivered in his belly. The goodbye with Rainey had been uneventful, and he and Henry had a quiet night at home. Things seemed a little too easy, but he'd enjoy it while it lasted.

Turning into the nearly empty church parking lot, Scott couldn't help but let a swell of pride draw his lips into a grin. Maybe his team had lost the baseball tournament, but with Henry's changed attitude, they had their choice of parking places. Not that the boy had been entirely compliant. He'd insisted on bringing his own coloring book instead of using the one the church provided. But it hadn't seemed like a battle worth fighting, since they were going to be early.

Instead of honking the horn to celebrate, Scott settled for holding up his hand for a high five. "Way to go, man. We're early. Grandma will be so proud."

"Yeah." Henry smacked Scott's palm. "We can get the front row."

"We'll see." One of the coveted spots on the last pew seemed like a better reward. Scott hopped out of his seat and collapsed it before Henry executed his new trick of climbing over the console and out the passenger door. "If you continue to be so good and sit still and quiet during church, there might be a special treat for you." The authors of the parenting blogs might frown upon bribery, but in his experience, albeit what little he had, positive reinforcement seemed to be a very effective strategy for achieving desired behavior.

Henry jumped from the running board and flew up the sidewalk. "Hurry up, Uncle Scott." With all his might, the little boy yanked on the handle of the sanctuary door but it barely budged until someone inside opened it.

"Well, good morning, Henry. It certainly is nice to see a child so excited about church." Mr. Gerald, one of the church leaders, held the door as Henry darted through. "Too bad about that loss, Coach, but I suppose we can't win 'em all."

"Yes, sir, but I sure plan to win more." Gritting his teeth, Scott entered the sanctuary. Henry stood in the middle of the aisle, scanning the congregation. No doubt, he was looking for Rainey, but Scott didn't see her.

Henry peered up at Scott. "Where's Rainey?"

"Maybe she's running late." Scott's stomach knotted. Until this moment, he'd successfully banished their last conversation from his thoughts. Maybe he'd been too hard on her, but he'd been exhausted and emotionally drained. Still, he'd gone too far. He'd apologize when she got here. Maybe treat her to another ice cream before she left. Everything would be fine. Taking Henry by the shoulder, Scott guided him into the front pew, but Mrs. Ellen appeared a few minutes later without Rainey.

"Good morning." She cut Scott a side-eye as she sat beside Henry.

"I made Rainey a soccer card with Sue's help." Henry pulled a piece of purple construction paper from inside the coloring book. "Where is she?"

"Oh, honey. Rainey decided to leave early this morning

instead of this afternoon. She said she thought it would be best, but I'll mail her your card." Mrs. Ellen took the paper. "That was very sweet of you."

Henry shook his head slowly, and wore a blank expression devoid of the brightness that had existed in his eyes only seconds before.

Scott swallowed the lump that'd formed in his throat. What had he done?

As the service progressed, Henry shrunk into himself, his skin growing paler as he stared with sad eyes at nothing. He didn't even flinch when Mrs. Ellen invited him to children's church. All the progress they'd made—gone.

Scott had known better than to let Rainey get too close, let Henry rely on her when they all knew she wasn't staying. But he'd been so happy, and who else knew the recipes that brought Henry to the table and how to coach soccer? For the first time since the funeral, it hadn't felt like they were living in a thick fog of grief. There had been laughter, and he'd hoped Henry would finally be okay with just him. After all, it hadn't been all Rainey. Scott and the boy had bonded and learned to live together in a healthier way.

If only Rainey hadn't already left. Surely, she understood how this would hurt Henry. While he might have told her not to draw things out, he hadn't thought she'd really leave without a final goodbye. It's not like this was the first time they'd argued, but he should've anticipated her reaction. Running is what she did when things got hard. Sure, he could've been more careful with his words, but her problem was with him, not Henry.

"Let us pray." Apparently, Pastor Tim had finished his sermon.

Scott bowed his head with the rest of the congregation, but Henry looked straight ahead. Being here wasn't helping, and Scott wanted to talk to him alone. They'd come so far, and they weren't going back. Scott would find a solution, but he couldn't do it with his parents interfering or anyone else. He'd certainly learned that lesson the hard way.

As Pastor continued his prayer, Scott scooped up Henry and fled the church, halting the tears that threatened to reveal his own sorrow.

Rainey dropped her backpack on the floor inside her extended-stay hotel room and collapsed face-first onto her bed. Her hamstring shrieked in anguish, but her tired body felt too heavy to lift to retrieve her ice pack. A week of training reminded her of the fierce competition between the best players of the game. She hadn't actually forgotten about the competition, more like convinced herself that it wasn't that bad, that her teammates were her friends, but the truth was, when it came to claiming a spot on the roster, it was every woman for herself.

Groaning, she rolled onto her back and gazed out of the window. Wisps of clouds glowed orange over the bright blue evening sky. Her stomach grumbled, but the last thing she wanted to do was stand in the small kitchen and prepare food. Actually, standing at all was something she'd pass on, but she'd come too far, given up too much, to quit now.

If only she could get a good night's sleep, but instead she awoke in a cold sweat with her pulse racing from nightmares about Henry being lost in the woods or, worse, drowning in the river. Only after she'd checked her phone to make sure there were no messages about Henry and told her irrational brain that Henry was safe could she calm her nerves and fall asleep as she prayed for the sweet boy. Almost as bad were the torturous, delightful dreams of strolling on the beach with Scott until he abandoned her and disappeared into the dunes.

Her early mornings left her body heavy with regret over her departure, over the finality, over the loneliness. But as she stepped onto the dew-covered field, the exhilaration of her dreams filled her with the energy to fight for her spot. The adrenaline didn't wane, her muscles didn't even twinge, until she trudged to her room at the end of the day.

But then, the night came again. Was she happy or sad? Hopeful or dejected?

"Lord, please give me strength." She limped to the freezer. Life could be worse. She could be sharing a hotel room with no kitchen or sleeping on an air mattress on a current player's floor, but her dad had insisted on paying for her own room. She'd be fine once she iced her hamstring and ate something. She knew better than to let her blood sugar get this low. With her ice pack tucked under her arm, she grabbed the protein drink she'd prepared on Sunday. "Thank You, God."

Rainey's phone rang and her heart skipped an unwarranted beat. It wouldn't be Scott. She'd made sure of that. As fast as she could hobble with her hands full, she made her way to the bed and answered the phone.

"Hi. How are things going?" Kayce asked.

"Okay, I guess." Rainey switched her phone to speaker and placed it beside her.

"What do you mean, you guess? Where is the confident Rainey I know?"

"I'm doing my best, but I can't read the coaches." After sliding a pillow under her ankles, Rainey situated the ice pack. "I felt like I was ready, but my hamstring is giving me fits. I've had some good plays. But I don't know if it will be enough."

"All you can do is play your game. If it doesn't work out with this team, then it wasn't the right place for you. That being said, if you're sore after training—and I know how you prepared—then you're leaving it all on the field."

"But some of these girls have amazing foot skills and ball control."

"Coaches notice everything, including passion and athleticism. So maybe your skills could improve. They can work with that, but they can't give a player passion. Trust the process."

"I'm trying, and I think I'm having fun. It's just hard knowing how long and hard I've worked for this chance, and it might not be enough."

"Remember what I said and don't try to be perfect. Have fun. Be fearless."

Fearless. With a sigh, Rainey dropped her head on the pillows, studying the ceiling. Why weren't the answers ever there? The only way she could play without fear is if she knew she was perfect. Every mistake haunted her, fueling her doubt, but there was no sense telling Kayce that, especially when she was in pep-talk mode.

"I hear you." She rolled her eyes—Rainey had given the polite response.

"We believe in you, Rainey, but I can sense your eyes rolling, so I'll take a hint. But know we are praying for you."

"Thanks, and Kayce, I do appreciate the support and encouragement. I'm just, well, everything… Anyway, what's going on with you?" Rainey sipped her drink.

"Not much. We're enjoying married life, which still feels unbelievable. I can't tell you how happy I am. After I turned thirty-five, I pretty much gave up on getting married, but God really surprised me. Just when I thought I had it all figured out, God changed everything. And it just feels like I'm right where I'm supposed to be. You know?"

"Sure." But Rainey's stomach twisted. Was this where she was supposed to be?

"Anyway, I'll let you go. John said he'd catch up with you tomorrow. Rainey, remember God's the same in the dark and the light. Just take it one day at a time and be courageous. You've got this."

After ending the call, Rainey collapsed over her legs and reached for her ankles, slowly allowing her tight muscles to stretch. Why was she questioning her place in this world? She should never have kissed Scott. That's when she'd lost her focus. One kiss, while amazing, couldn't change her life's direction. But it wasn't just the kiss. Scott was her friend—honest and true and thoughtful. Maybe her feelings for him were strong, but he'd pushed her away. She understood he needed to protect Henry, so she accepted that this was where she was supposed to be. Scott was where he was supposed to be, and it wasn't with her.

As Scott finished his supper, his gaze landed on Henry, who stared into a bowl of artificially flavored cereal. He trailed the spoon through the shapes, creating swirls of colors in the rainbow-tinted milk. It'd been one week since Rainey left, and Henry had barely mumbled a sentence to him, but the short time felt like eternity. Scott had even made one of Rainey's recipes, but Henry refused the food.

Scott carried his dishes to the sink. "After you finish your cereal, we can drive over to the field and kick the ball."

"At what? You took down the goal." Henry scooped two of the shapes onto his spoon.

Scott winced, but at least Henry was talking. "We needed the field for baseball, but we could work on your dribbling and passing." He rinsed his plate and loaded it in the dishwasher.

"I don't want to play soccer. It's stupid."

"We don't use that word."

"Why not?" Henry glared. He was being disrespectful, but he was also showing some emotion, which was a step in the right direction.

Scott furrowed his fingers through his hair. During square dance, Mrs. Mayfield had told a student not to use the word, but why? Obviously, it wasn't nice to call people names, but Henry was talking about a game, so was it okay? Were there exceptions to this rule?

"It isn't nice." *Pitiful.* Scott reached for the bowl of mushy, bloated cereal. "Are you finished with this?"

"I guess." Henry plopped his spoon in the milk.

"Buddy, we can't keep going on like this." He'd thought that by now, Henry would be ready to move on. He'd only known Rainey a short time.

But then again, it'd been long enough to leave his uncle's heart splintered. How had she become such an important part of their lives in such a short period of time?

Sighing, he dumped the cereal mash down the drain. Logically, he knew Rainey's happiness was the most important thing, and he should be happy for her, but he couldn't convince his heart. How could he blame the kid? If he was honest with himself, he'd admit that all he really wanted was to take back all his stupid words to her. And there was no better adjective to describe what he'd said. They'd probably still be talking if he hadn't been so, well, stupid. Good thing Henry couldn't hear his thoughts, and he could beat himself up later, but right now, he needed to help Henry.

Scott took his seat at the table. "I know you're sad about Rainey leaving, but she's getting the chance to play with a great team. I thought you were excited for her. Isn't that why you made her the card?"

"I wanted to give it to her."

"Mrs. Ellen said she'd mail it."

"I wanted to give it to Rainey."

"I'm sorry."

Henry's brow wrinkled with confusion. "It's your fault?"

"No, I mean—" Scott's throat constricted, stopping his words. But it was his fault.

Henry's eyes grew round as he waited for his uncle's explanation.

Scott had to do something to make this right. His heart thumped hard against his tight chest as his mind searched through empty files for a solution other than the one that involved his phone, but it was the only answer. With unmerited courage, Scott set it on the table. "We could call her."

"Can we do it with the picture?"

"Um." Retreating from the phone, Scott scratched his stubble. "Maybe I should text first and be sure she's available, and we need to walk Champ, and you need to take a bath."

Henry pushed the phone across the table, thrusting out his bottom lip. "Please, can we call Rainey first? Puh-lease."

"Okay." Scott drummed his fingers on the phone's screen. What would he say? Would she even take his call? She would for Henry, and he was the one so desperate to call her. Scott shuffled to the counter. His mom had made a batch of Rainey's muffins and delivered them on Thursday, but Henry had refused to look at them, much less eat one. Surely a couple of these supernutritious muffins could make up for a few days of Henry's sugary cereal consumption. Scott placed two muffins in front of his headstrong nephew. "I'll text Rainey as soon as you eat those muffins and have a cup of milk." With an eye trained on Henry, Scott grabbed the jug from the refrigerator.

"Okay." Henry shoved half of the muffin in his mouth. "I wove deese mufwins."

Shaking his head, Scott resisted the urge to tell the boy

not to talk with food in his mouth, but he couldn't hold down the wave of pride swelling within him. He'd successfully bought some time to gather his thoughts before talking with Rainey, and he'd managed to get some healthy food in Henry. He carried a cup of milk to Henry, who'd already devoured one of the muffins and started on the next. At this rate, his time wouldn't last much longer. He should have gone for three muffins.

Clutching the phone, Scott paced the kitchen while typing.

Hi, Rainey. It's Scott and Henry.

No. She'd already know it was him. He erased the words as he pivoted at the sink and headed to the table, typing another message that began with an apology, but that didn't seem like something he should text. He smashed Delete as he turned around and started another message.

"All done." Henry slammed his cup onto the table. "Did you send the text? What did she say?"

Scott erased his most recent version. He shouldn't bother Rainey, but Henry gazed at him with bright eyes and a smile he hadn't seen in too long. Scott stared at the screen, his finger hovering above the keyboard. *And this was supposed to be the easy part.* What would he do when she was looking at him?

Scott stopped and exhaled sharply. "Help me, God." As fast as possible, he typed out the message.

Can you do a video chat? Henry wants to say hi.

Holding his breath and cringing until he could barely see the screen, Scott pressed Send. As the seconds slipped by, he slowly opened one eye and then the other. Nothing. Not even those little dots that meant she was typing. Maybe God was granting him a reprieve. Another minute went by, and he rolled his shoulders. "Henry, I guess she can't do it. How about we take Champ for a walk or toss him the ball in the backyard?"

Buzz.

Scott's heart seized as he gripped the phone. *So close.*

Sure. Now?

Short and sweet. So why had it taken so long for her to respond?

"What'd she say?" Henry bounced beside Scott. "Did she say yes?" He yanked on Scott's forearm. "Uncle Scott."

"Just a minute, buddy." Scott sent a message, asking if the time worked for her, and within a heartbeat, now that his heart had started working again, she responded that she was free and would send a link. Great. He pocketed his phone. "Go get my laptop and meet me in the living room."

"Yes!" Henry punched his fists in the air as he ran into the dining room.

This was happening. As he made his way to the couch, Scott's nerves dug a hole in his stomach. He did want to see Rainey, but did she want to see him? It didn't matter. He didn't matter. What mattered was Henry, and if Scott could do this small thing for his nephew, he would.

Henry gave Scott the computer. "This'll be so great. My friend Justin says he plays games on the computer with his grandparents who live in North Carolina. Can we do that, too?"

"We'll see." Scott navigated to his email. "We need to remember that Rainey might only have a few minutes." Even if she didn't ask for it, he knew Rainey needed to focus on her game, so he'd make sure they weren't a distraction.

While the computer flashed various messages on their way to the meeting room, Scott's heartbeat intensified as if he was running to first, and an outfielder overthrew the first baseman, so he rounded the base, but wasn't quite sure he'd be safe at second, so he slid into the bag—

Rainey's beautiful smile and slate-blue eyes filled the screen. "Hi, guys."

Safe. Scott could almost hear the umpire call, his heart still sprinting, but with the awareness that he was winning in this moment.

Chapter Twelve

"Hi," Scott said. Had his face brightened?

Rainey stared, entrapped by those brown eyes as time seemed to slow. A slight blush crept along the edge of his beard as the corners of his lips lifted slightly.

Rainey's heart did somersaults as she tried to manage her expression, but she was unable to divert her gaze from Scott's. Had she sounded casual? She'd rehearsed the greeting while she'd waited for them to connect. She was going for bright and happy, but the way the corners of her mouth were pressing into her cheeks, she may have crept over the edge to a goofy grin.

She'd worked off most of her frustration with him at trainings, so she knew she could be cordial, but seeing Scott intensified everything.

Just remember the meeting is for Henry, just Henry, only Henry. Henry, Henry, Henry.

But as Scott disappeared from view, her tumbling heart landed with a thud of disappointment. Rainey locked her molars, holding her smile in place. This was ridiculous. Scott didn't text her to spend time with her. He'd made it clear that whatever they'd shared was taped off and safely in the friend zone. Besides, she adored Henry and wanted to see him. Unfortunately, her logical, efficient brain could not convince the rest of her body from reacting to Scott's presence.

Henry beamed, waving. "Hi, Rainey."

On seeing the happy boy, warmth covered any inkling of disappointment. Relaxing against her pillows, Rainey crossed her ankles. "How are things going? I'm sorry I didn't see you again before I left, but I got your card." She slipped the folded piece of construction paper from her bedside table and held it up to the camera. "Thank you for making it for me." Receiving the sweet message from Henry had been exactly what she needed in the middle of the week when she didn't think she'd make it to Friday night.

Henry clapped. "Are you scoring lots of goals? Will you be on TV? Can we come to a game?"

"I've scored a few goals." But not nearly enough. Not to mention she'd been out-skilled way too many times. "I'm not sure if I'll be on TV or if there will be a game that you can come to. I might be going overseas for another season."

"I thought we'd get to see you play." Henry scrunched his brow as his focus drifted to where Scott must be sitting.

"I hope you will someday." Rainey placed the card beside her. "Tell me what you've been up to."

"Nothing." Henry's chin fell.

"We haven't had the best week." Scott's arm dropped around Henry, and the scene in the picture shifted again, bringing Scott into view and a flutter to her traitorous heart.

"Uh-oh. Champ didn't get out again?"

"No, we fixed the fence on Sunday afternoon." Scott squeezed Henry's shoulder. "And Mom brought over a batch of your muffins."

"I'm so glad she could bake them for you. Henry, are you making sure to eat healthy so you can grow to be stronger than your uncle and beat him in all the sports, even baseball?"

Henry shot his uncle a challenge, his frown quirking into

a sly smile. "I'm going to be so much faster and stronger than Uncle Scott."

"You'll have to train hard and eat right and get lots of sleep."

"Yes, ma'am." Wiggling out of Scott's embrace, Henry sat up straight. "You know what else?" He bounced, tossing a smirk at Scott, like he was about to remind him who was boss.

"What?" she asked cautiously, not wanting Henry's efforts to please her to upset Scott's authority.

"I'm going to be a batboy for the baseball team." Henry crossed his arms over his chest.

"You are?" Scott cocked an eyebrow, giving his nephew the side-eye. "But you said… Actually, never mind."

Henry must've been giving him a hard time. Poor Scott. Everything he did was to make that little boy happy. Hopefully, one day Henry would realize it.

"Just like Rainey said, I'll be better than you at all the sports." Henry nodded.

"Wow. You'll be the best batboy ever." She pointed at the screen. "Henry, I think it would be great for you to play lots of different sports. Your uncle is a great coach. He almost taught me to hit the ball." Hopefully, they couldn't see the heat pricking her cheeks.

"I think if we'd had another lesson, you'd have hit it out of the park." Scott spared her that aggravatingly adorable lopsided grin, clearly not bothered by Henry's motivations enough to keep from teasing her.

"Can you teach me to hit out of the park?" Henry asked.

Scott jerked his attention from her, looking down at the little boy who was looking right at him. Finally. If Rainey was one of the girls who cried at greeting-card commercials, this picture of adoration would've done her in.

"Are you saying you want to play baseball?" Scott focused solely on Henry.

Henry nodded. "Daddy gave me a bat and a glove for my birthday."

Tears welled in Rainey's eyes, and Scott dabbed his finger under his. They'd be alright—better than alright—and they didn't need her. Scott was a great dad. It was time for her to let them go.

"Hey, guys. It's time for me to get ready for bed. I'm so glad you're going to play baseball, Henry. You'll be great." She forced her trembling lips upward.

They both turned to the camera with the same expression. She'd never noticed how much Henry resembled Scott, but it wasn't only their appearance. Their manners were similar in a way that happens with parents and children. It always irked her when people said she sounded like her mom, but seeing it on these two gave her hope for their relationship.

"Tell Rainey good-night," Scott said.

Henry punched his arms across his chest. "I thought we were going to play a game."

"Rainey has to get a good night's sleep. We want her to play her best tomorrow. Don't we?"

"Yes, but—"

"No *buts*, and it's getting late for us, too. Bu-u-u-t—" Scott dragged out the word "—if you get ready for bed quickly, we can read an extra book."

Perfect play, Scott. Rainey's heart swelled.

"Fine." Henry leaned close to the screen. "Rainey, can we play a game next time?" he whispered.

"We'll see." She caught her lip under her teeth. She hated being noncommittal, but uncertainty seemed to be the only constant in her life.

Scott replaced Henry and said, "Thanks for talking to him

and thank you for everything you did when you were here. I'm sorry I was such a fool before you left. I have no excuse."

"You'd just lost a tournament and Henry in one afternoon. Don't be so hard on yourself. If I hadn't thought you were right, I wouldn't have listened to you."

"Still, I'm sorry. You've always been so great with Henry. He really misses you, especially your food."

What about you? Do you miss me? I didn't even know my heart could react like this, but you don't seem fazed. Meanwhile, her emotions swung between extremes.

She highlighted the end button. "I've missed him, too, but y'all seem to be doing okay. I'll email you my recipe book." Her finger hovered over the mouse. "Give Henry a hug for me. Good night."

"Good night, Rainey. I hope you get your dream."

Rainey tapped the end button and let the tears spill. If this was how love felt, she'd rather be slid into cleats-up.

Scott closed Henry's bedroom door and trudged to the living-room couch. He'd almost made it five days since their video call. A busy schedule was good for something, but with the clicking of the wall clock—the only thing breaking the silence—his shoulders yielded to the weight of despair. Closing his eyes and inhaling deeply, he could almost smell Rainey's citrus scent and feel the warmth of her arms wrapped around him. While he may have doubted how much he cared for her, two weeks apart and not knowing when he might see her again had made it clear that his feelings for her were not only different, but also stronger than he'd ever known. All his past relationships paled in comparison.

On the coffee table, his phone tempted him. Rainey didn't say he shouldn't call. But other than the email with her recipes, she hadn't reached out. Of course, it probably didn't help he'd ended the call professing how much Henry missed her. Regret scraped at the pit of his stomach. The only word in her email was *enjoy*. Not even a "hi, how you doing?" But what did he expect? She was busy living her best life, and they, well, they were living their best lives, too, but it didn't stop the pangs of longing and loneliness.

What would she think if he called? Did he really care? Lifting the phone, he slid his thumb across the screen. What he needed was an excuse. Or maybe not. Wasn't that his whole problem? At the very least, they were friends. His heart shuttered at the description of their relationship, but friends did check in on each other. Before he could talk himself out of it, like he'd done every other night, Scott pressed Send.

With each tone, his pulse accelerated like he was shifting into a higher gear in his jeep. Maybe she wouldn't answer, but then did he leave a message or send a text? This shouldn't be so complicated, which further proved it meant more. He'd never given a second thought to calling a woman he was interested in. Another tone sounded. How many was that?

"Hi," Rainey answered, sounding breathless. "Sorry, I couldn't find my phone. Is everything okay?"

"Hi, yes, I, um—" He kneaded his skull. What was he going to say?

"Did Henry convince you to call me again?"

Henry? No, no. Had he really been hiding behind a five-year-old? Scott slapped his palm to his forehead. *Stupid, stupid, stupid man!* Why would anyone suggest eliminating the word?

"Scott? Are you there?"

"Yes, uh, sorry. I was just calling to check in, since we hadn't heard from you."

"I'm good…tired."

"Same, but in a good way. We spend most of our time at

the baseball field between the high-school team and Henry's practices." Once Henry showed interest in baseball, Scott registered him for T-ball. "Believe it or not, Henry was so zonked, he didn't even ask for a story tonight. Just cuddled up with Champ and fell asleep." Scott clamped his jaw. *Stop talking about Henry.* But didn't all parents talk about their kids? *Yes, but not to the woman they wanted to kiss.*

"I'm sure you love playing baseball with him."

"If you mean instead of soccer, you'll be happy to know, we're planning to resume soccer after the high-school season wraps."

"I didn't, but that's fantastic," she said matter-of-factly.

"It is. I always figured I'd be coaching my kids, but I didn't expect it to be so soon."

"How are you holding up?"

"Actually, I like coaching, both Henry and at the high school, way more than I expected. It's fulfilling in a completely different way than playing." He stretched out his legs on the table and crossed his ankles. It was so nice talking to someone who understood his conflicting emotions and wouldn't judge him, but she sounded a little detached.

"That's great. I'm glad you're happy." Another polite answer.

"Don't get me wrong, I'm still getting used to the idea of this being my future."

"I'm sure it will take some time." Her answers felt more like she was his therapist instead of his friend.

"Yeah, but honestly, when Henry hit that first ball, it felt so right, like someone had glued a huge piece of my heart in its place." He cringed. "That sounded so corny."

"Maybe a little, but also very sweet." Finally, she was sounding a little like herself.

"You're sweet for not making fun of me. You must be really tired."

"Ha ha. Maybe so, but I'm also feeling nostalgic, which is weird because none of this is a part of my past. For whatever reason, when I think about Woodley, it feels like what home is supposed to feel like. I can't believe I said that. I mean if you'd told eleven-year-old me that I would consider Woodley home, I might have stomped on your foot."

"I'm pretty sure eleven-year-old you did stomp on my foot." Maybe he shouldn't have made the joke, but that's what they did. He'd missed the authenticity of their conversations.

"Truth." Rainey's laughter flooded him with warmth and washed away the awkwardness between them. "Thanks for calling. I've missed this."

"Me, too. Although I do have Henry's daily reports from kindergarten, it's nice to talk to an adult. I'm used to having a team of guys to hang out with."

"And I imagine a few ladies," she teased.

"Occasionally."

"Believe it or not, I haven't ever really had a close friend."

"Hank was my best friend. We talked almost every day. I think that's what I miss the most."

"I'm so sorry, Scott."

"No, it's fine. Don't apologize." He smacked his leg. Way to bring down the mood. "We said from the beginning that we would be completely honest. In fact, we shook on it."

"The truth, even if it hurts…" Rainey's voice trailed off like she was realizing her words held a lot more meaning now than they had then. She'd probably rolled her lip between her teeth.

At the vision of her lips, the chance of another kiss flew at him like a fastball, but he swung and missed. He rubbed his sweaty palm on his leg. If he didn't want to strike out, he needed to tell her how he felt, and it had to be in person.

But when would he even see her again? Maybe her distance was for the best, so he wouldn't act on his emotions and say something they'd all regret. He couldn't ask her to give up on her dreams for him. If she made the decision herself, it would be a different story, but for now, he needed to stop thinking about kissing and be content with friendship or maybe he needed to let her go all together—

"Scott…"

"Sorry, I got lost in my thoughts. Guess I need to go to bed."

"Me, too." She yawned. "See you later."

As Scott put down his phone, her words needled him. *See you later.* But it was just a figure of speech.

After staying up too late analyzing every word of his conversation with Rainey like it was game film, Saturday morning arrived too soon, but Scott couldn't sleep in. Today was the community-wide celebration kicking off baseball season, and the parade through town was an annual tradition.

Scott scraped whole-wheat flour off a measuring cup and dumped it in the mixing bowl, ignoring the pit of gloom in his stomach. Maybe with time, contentment would fill the void Rainey had left, but his impulsive phone call only prolonged his suffering.

"Here's the milk, chef." Henry slid the jug onto the counter. "I love Rainey's banana, chocolate-chip pancakes."

"Me, too, buddy." Scott poured the milk into a measuring cup. "Are you excited about the parade?"

"Yes. I loved the Christmas parade. I got lots of candy. Do you think Rainey will come to the Christmas parade?"

"I don't know." Scott screwed the lid on the milk jug. "Put the milk in the fridge."

"Do you think Rainey is making pancakes or muffins for breakfast?"

"I'm sure it's something healthy."

"I think muffins." Henry grabbed the jug. "I used to help Mommy make breakfast for Daddy, and we would surprise him and have a breakfast picnic on their bed."

"That sounds fun." Scott scooped a heaping tablespoon of brown sugar. Since Henry had asked to play baseball, he'd talked more about his parents. At first Scott worried that he might regress, but they'd found comfort in their memories of Hank and Kristen. More importantly, Scott had released a lot of guilt. Rainey was right. He couldn't keep blaming himself.

Henry climbed up on the stool and stirred the batter. "Rainey would be a good mom."

Scott gasped, his abs contracting like he'd taken a fastball to the belly. Maybe when Rainey had been at their house, he'd let himself imagine a life with her, but he'd always known it was impossible, and nothing had changed. He moved his head slowly from side to side, cracking the tight muscles in his neck. While it was a nice thought and he could manage it, he needed to be sure Henry wasn't banking on Rainey's return.

"Buddy, I'm sure Rainey will make a good mom, but I don't know when she'll visit. Woodley isn't her home." Even if she thought of it that way. Leaning around Henry, Scott tossed in a pinch of salt. "Remember, she was only here to visit her grandparents, and we want her to make the team. That's her dream."

"I wish she could be on a soccer team in Woodley."

"Me, too." Scott clanked the skillet on the stove.

"If Rainey decided to be a mom instead of a soccer player, could she be my mom? Then we could all live here together."

Scott fumbled the spatula but caught it before it hit the floor. "Henry, I'll start cooking these. Go put on your uniform. We don't want to be late."

"Okay." Henry climbed down from the chair. "Uncle Scott, if Rainey doesn't make the team, we should ask her if she wants to be a mom."

Scott tightened his grip on the handle. His brain knew it was impossible, even if his heart and his nephew didn't want to believe it. "I think she's going to play for another team."

"But don't you think it would be fun if she were my mom and lived here with us?"

"Of course, I do." Scott winced. How had he let that slip out? "But it isn't going to happen."

"Not if we don't ask her."

"Henry, how would we even ask her? She isn't here." Scott slapped a pat of butter on the skillet.

"But if she's here…"

"If that ever happened, somehow I doubt I'd be able to stop you from asking her." Scott pointed the spatula at the boy. "Now, go get dressed and let's focus on something that might actually happen today like playing T-ball."

"Yes, sir." Henry hurried to his room, while Scott poured the batter on the skillet.

Would Rainey ever consider retiring from professional soccer? Henry was right—she would make a great mom, and who knew, she probably would one day, but he needed to face reality. That day was not anytime soon.

After filling their bellies with pancakes, Scott and Henry met his team at city hall before they marched down Main Street to the baseball fields. The younger kids shared a field behind the high-school stadium. No doubt, this town needed more fields.

Strolling down the road, Henry held Scott's hand as they

waved to his grandparents stationed in front of the hardware store. The same place they'd stood when Hank held his hand in their first parade. Grief clenched his chest.

Hank should be the one walking with his son. They should be making memories together. Would every milestone in Henry's life be met with this moment of realization? Even as Scott hoped to keep Henry happy, he wanted him to remember his parents. He wanted them to always be a part of Henry's life.

Rainey was right. He couldn't replace his brother. They'd always been the best teammates, Hank on the pitcher's mound, and Scott at first base. While they were identical in lots of ways, it was how they complemented each other that made them a formidable duo. Scott needed to protect first base, but he couldn't be the pitcher, too. Hank had mastered his roles, and Scott could master his, as coach, as teacher and, most importantly, as Henry's father. While he might not do exactly what Hank would've done, Scott's choices would always be influenced by his brother.

"Rainey." Henry waved wildly. "She's here."

"It must be someone who looks like her." Scott scanned the crowd. He'd been in such a daze he hadn't noticed that they were almost to the fields.

"It's her. See?" Henry pointed.

Scott's heart skittered as his gaze landed on Rainey. With a bright smile, she gave a small wave. How was she here? More importantly, what did it mean?

"Come on." Henry pulled on Scott's wrist. "I want to tell her about my game."

As they covered the short distance, Scott tried to order his thoughts, but electricity shot through his nerves, overloading his senses.

Henry wrapped his arms around Rainey's waist. "I missed you so much."

"I missed you, too, buddy." Rainey returned the hug. "Surprise?" Her voice drew up like she wasn't sure.

"More like shock." Scott laughed, hoping to set her at ease even if energy was pumping through him at an alarming rate.

Henry jumped out of the embrace. "Can you come to my game?"

"I think so." She shifted to Scott, lifting her brows.

"Of course, you should come unless you have somewhere else you need to be…"

"Not at the moment. I borrowed Grandpa's truck to drive to the tryout, so I needed to return it. Kayce is coming later to take me to Jacksonville. My grandparents couldn't drive me with Palm Sunday tomorrow and Holy week."

"Oh, right." Scott scratched the bristle on his chin. "Makes sense." But did it really? He had so many questions. Did that mean she'd made the team? He wanted to talk to her. He needed to talk to her. But could he ask her the hard question? One thing at a time. He wouldn't do anything to jeopardize her career.

"The parade was a bit of a surprise, though." Rainey shot a look at her grandmother.

"I'm sure. The game's at eleven thirty, so we better head to the field." Scott clapped Henry's shoulder. "Ready, buddy?"

"Have fun!" Rainey called as they fell back in line with the parade of players. If Rainey stuck around after the game, he'd talk to her, but only to find out her plans.

As Rainey and Grandma found spots on the bleachers, Scott jogged to the center of the field, stopping between home plate and the pitcher's mound. Before the children used the tee to hold the baseball, he pitched two balls to them. If they missed both, they used the tee. After each player batted, most of the kids in the field rushed to the ball, resulting in several pileups. Clearly, she wouldn't learn the rules of the game watching this modified version, but it warmed her heart when Henry waved to her as he strutted to home plate. After barely missing the first ball, he connected with the second and dashed to first base.

While Rainey cheered, her gaze fell on Scott. He beamed with pride, running a finger under his eye. Maybe his life wasn't what he'd planned, but he would never forget this moment. Watching Scott and Henry heal and grow together under the worst of circumstances had changed her, but what did she do now? Maybe a couple of days here would give her clarity, or maybe she'd just cause herself, and probably others, more pain. She chewed her lip, trying to concentrate on the game and not the coach.

When all the children had a chance to bat twice, the game ended. As the players lined up and slapped hands, Rainey skipped down the bleachers. When Henry approached her, she gave him a high five. "Great game. I was so impressed that you hit the ball both times."

"I've been practicing with Uncle Scott," Henry said.

"He's a great coach."

Scott nudged her. "I couldn't teach you."

"Well, maybe you need to give me another lesson." As her cheeks enflamed, she clamped her lips together before blurting anything else.

"Anytime." He fixed his gaze on her, holding her captive.

"Great game, boys! Why don't y'all join us for lunch?" Grandma's voice broke the trance, and Rainey snapped her attention from Scott. "The barbeque smells delicious."

"Yes!" Henry punched a fist in the air.

"Thank you. We'd love to join y'all."

"Wonderful." Grandma caught Henry's hand and guided him toward the food tent.

Scott leaned close to Rainey's ear. "I guess that means we're postponing the batting lesson." His warm breath tickled her neck, spreading goose bumps over her skin.

She snatched the end of her ponytail and twisted it around her fingers. Was he flirting? Because he didn't seem to be talking about batting. But then again, what if he was?

"Rainey, relax. I was kidding." Scott's hand covered hers, but if he meant to calm her nerves, he was only making it worse. Her skin crawled with a terrible mix of humiliation and excitement.

"Of course. I know. I think I just need to eat." She slipped her hand free and jogged to catch up to Henry.

Scott slung his gear bag over his shoulder and followed Henry and Rainey. Was she mad at him? She'd started it with that comment about him being a great coach. He'd almost let himself believe she was thinking about staying for a while, at least long enough for a batting lesson. *Foolish heart.* He still didn't even know if she'd made the team.

Henry gave Scott a mischievous grin before he gazed up at Rainey with adoration. "Rainey, do you want to be a mom?"

No. Scott's pulse skidded to a stop, but Henry hadn't asked her to be his mom. It wasn't too late.

"Great question, Henry," Mrs. Ellen chuckled.

After Rainey silenced her grandmother with a stern look, she turned her attention to the little boy. "I think so. Someday."

Before Henry asked his follow-up question, Scott picked up his pace, edging himself between Mrs. Ellen and his inquisitive nephew. "Henry, did you tell Rainey about the Easter egg hunt?"

"No," Henry said, screwing up his face.

Seriously? The kid hadn't stopped talking about the golden egg all week, but now, he thought it was an odd topic.

Rainey glanced between the two of them like she was deciding whose side to take. *Please let it be mine.* But she settled her eyes on Henry. "When is it?"

"Tomorrow after church. I'm going to find one of the golden eggs and get lots of candy. We're having a picnic, and the Easter Bunny might even come."

Under the tent, they stopped in front of the drink station, and Mrs. Ellen began filling cups with ice and lemonade. "I heard the Easter Bunny will definitely be there." Smirking, she gave cups to Scott and Rainey. "Y'all look like you could use a cold drink."

Rainey pressed the cup to her cheek. "It was hot in the sun."

"Yeah. It must be ten degrees cooler in the shade." Scott gulped the lemonade.

"Henry, let's go order the food." Mrs. Ellen gave the boy his drink and whispered something in his ear. "We can meet y'all back at the house."

"Yes, ma'am." Henry hustled to the food line.

"We can help," Rainey offered.

"Don't be silly." Mrs. Ellen gave Scott a pointed look.

"Thanks. I need to clean up before we eat." Scott grabbed his bag and pressed his fingers against Rainey's back. Normally, he wouldn't go along with Mrs. Ellen's scheming but if he wanted to talk to Rainey alone, this might be his only chance. "Ready?"

"It doesn't seem I have a choice." She shrugged.

"You always have a choice. If you want to wait, we can."

Rainey hitched a thumb toward the parsonage. "Let's go."

Unfortunately, since he was the varsity baseball coach in a small town, it wasn't easy to get through a crowd on opening day. Scott kept the conversations as brief as possible while also being polite until they emerged on the other side. "Sorry about that." He held the gate to Rainey's grandparents' backyard.

"No worries. You're a very important person around here." She lowered onto a wicker chair at the table. The rays of the sun shot through the limbs of the magnolia, making her blond hair shimmer, and Scott's pulse quicken.

How should he start? Before she left, things had not been great between them, but today she was acting like they were old friends. He took a long slow drink and joined her. "The attention can be a lot, especially when you want to have a private conversation."

"We just had a private conversation last night."

"I prefer to talk in person."

"Me, too." But she averted her eyes, staring at something in the distance. "Henry seems to be doing well."

"He is, but I think we covered all things Henry and baseball last night." Scott brushed his hand over hers. "How are you? I'm getting the impression the tryout didn't go the way you'd hoped."

"I haven't actually heard, but I'm certain I won't be getting a call. I don't know what happened. I thought I was ready and focused, but every day was worse than the one before. And the worst part is I can't figure out what to do next or what I did wrong. Dad and Kayce want me to rest before we decide."

"Sounds like a good plan. So you're going to stay in Jacksonville?"

"That's the plan." She returned her focus to him.

Henry ran around the corner of the house. "We're going to decorate cookies!"

Rainey held Scott's gaze for another moment, raising her brow. Did she want him to ask her to stay?

He didn't want to cause her further confusion. She needed to figure this out on her own.

Mrs. Ellen rushed up behind Henry. "But first, we're going to wash those hands." She placed two bags of food on the table. "We'll be right back with more lemonade."

This wasn't how Scott wanted to have this conversation if they were really going to have it at all. He didn't want to rush her into any decisions when she had to be exhausted physically and emotionally. But he also didn't want to push her away when it seemed she might be close to deciding to retire. If he was going to confess his true feelings for her, he wanted her to be in the right mindset. But how long did he have?

Before Grandma could direct Henry into the house, he darted to Rainey and wrapped his arms around her neck. "I'm so glad you're here!"

"Me, too, buddy." She embraced him, relishing the warmth that filled her.

"Are you going to be on the soccer team?" Henry asked.

"I don't think so."

"If you aren't going to be on the team, why can't you stay here and be my coach?" Henry crossed his arms over his chest.

"I—I…" Rainey turned to Scott. What was she supposed to say? The kid had a point, and she didn't have an answer.

"Henry, leave Rainey alone." Scott rose and gripped his nephew's shoulder. "She has plans."

But she didn't have plans. For the first time in ten years, every minute wasn't scheduled and dedicated to reaching her goal of playing in the National Women's Soccer League. Not that she couldn't easily continue to train and play overseas and earn another opportunity to try out, but nothing was planned yet.

"I'm sorry, Henry." She wanted to say more, but she didn't want to give him false hope when her doubts clouded all her decisions.

"Let's hurry and get you washed up so you can spend as much time with Rainey as possible before she leaves." Grandma led Henry inside.

As they entered the house, Scott turned to Rainey. "When are you leaving?"

"Kayce's supposed to pick me up tomorrow night." Rainey stood and tugged at the knotted handles of the plastic food bags with her nerves misfiring. Was this really the end? They'd barely begun but was he even still interested? He'd said he was joking about the batting lesson, so did he not want to kiss her?

"Rainey, I don't want for us, for this—" He clutched the back of his head. "What I'm trying to say—" He trailed his fingers down her arm to her hand, where he kept his eyes focused. "We should keep in touch. We don't have to be strangers."

Strangers? "Okay. I don't want to be strangers, either." She studied him, a lump forming in her throat. Did he want to be friends, or more, or less? *Strangers?*

"Good, so we can keep in touch. Maybe do another video call with Henry."

"Sure." She slipped out of his hold and retreated a step. "With Henry." She loved Henry, but would their relationship only exist for Henry's benefit?

"That didn't out right."

Really? If only they had a signal for this communication like they had at the wedding. What did he want from her? Nothing made sense.

"I mean we can keep in touch, too. It doesn't always have to be with Henry." In one breath, Scott closed the space between them, and even though he didn't touch her, her skin warmed as if he was holding her. "Okay?"

"Okay." Hope filled her heart, even though everything remained uncertain. She bit down on her smile, trying to manage her expectations.

"We'll miss you." Scott encircled her waist, hugging her. "I'll miss you."

"Me, too." Rainey wrapped her arms around him, resting her head on his chest. "Thank you for being understanding."

"Of course. I just want you to be happy." He kissed the top of her head and then stepped away, letting his arms fall by his sides. "I should wash up, too."

Sunday morning, Rainey peeked around the curtains in her grandparents' living room as parents dropped off their children to line up for the Palm Sunday processional. She couldn't wait to see Scott's expression when he realized who was in the bunny costume. At first, she'd balked at her grandmother's idea, but the person who was supposed to do it had gotten the flu, and they were desperate, so she'd relented.

As Scott and Henry hurried to join the group on the sidewalk, Scott smoothed Henry's hair. Adorable. They both wore green-and-white-plaid button-down shirts with khaki shorts and boat shoes. Scott's mom must have chosen those outfits, and they were perfect. A teenage girl gave Henry a palm branch, while Scott strode into the sanctuary.

Once she saw the church door shut, Rainey slipped out of the parsonage and snuck up behind Henry. "Good morning."

"Rainey." Henry hugged her.

"I can't wait to hear you sing. After church I have a surprise for your uncle, and then we can spend the afternoon together."

"He's so happy you're home." Henry crouched closer to

her and used his palm branch to hide them. "He wants you to live here with us."

"What?" Rainey leaned closer, her pulse kicking up a notch. Surely, Henry had misunderstood.

"I told him to ask you to be my mom, but he didn't." Henry pouted.

"Henry, did he say he wanted me to be your mom?"

"I think so."

What did that mean?

"Boys and girls, it's time to march in." Grandma waved a palm branch above her head. "Wave your branches as we go and find your place on the riser. Sing out."

Fanning herself, Rainey watched the children disappear into the sanctuary. What would she say if Scott asked her to stay? With each step toward the door, she focused on her breathing. He wouldn't do that to her. He wouldn't make her choose. This new arrangement between them, whatever it was, may not be ideal, but he wouldn't press her for more. As strange as it sounded, that's why she could no longer imagine her life without him in it. He got her like no one else.

Following the last volunteer, Rainey slipped into the rear of the sanctuary. From his spot on the riser, Henry spotted her and waved. Being his mom certainly wouldn't be the worst thing. She waved as joy filled her heart. In fact, it would probably be one of the greatest things she'd ever done. If only it was as simple as Henry made it sound.

After the children finished their song, Rainey snuck out of the church and returned to the parsonage to don the bunny suit. The plan was for her to come in at the end of the service and escort the children to the egg hunt. Once in her room, she exchanged her sundress for a pair of running shorts and a tank. The costume was made of a thick material and the giant head only had small vents. With the rising temperature, she didn't want to put it on until the last minute.

After taking a long drink of cold water, she checked her phone for the time, then placed it on the dresser with her water bottle. She stepped into the costume and zipped it up before pulling on the ridiculous rabbit feet. Hopefully, she wouldn't trip. Peering through the screen of the bunny's mouth, she made her way to the back of the church.

As Rainey struggled with the door, it thrust forward and a blast of cold air blew through the vents of the costume, chilling Rainey's clammy skin.

"Do you need any help?" Scott peered into the bunny's mouth, meeting Rainey's gaze before she could look away. He squinted, scrutinizing her before his eyes grew wide with realization. "Rainey?" He almost smashed his face against the screen.

"Shhh. Don't let the children hear you." She worked to raise one of her gloved fingers to the bunny's mouth. "Surprise." She shoved him playfully. "You need to make some space. Someone will think there's something wrong with you, or worse, you're trying to kiss the Easter Bunny."

"Hmm, that doesn't sound so bad." He smirked.

"Stop it." She pressed her mitt against his shoulder, pushing him out of the way, but that didn't stop the tiny fireworks zipping inside her. "I can't be late, and I have no peripheral vision in this thing, so can you guide me to the sanctuary?"

He clasped the fluffy glove. "This is absolutely not how I thought this morning would go."

Giddiness bubbled in Rainey. It was fun to be silly. "I wanted to surprise you later, but I'm glad you rescued me."

"Anytime, but I hope we can hang out without the costume before you leave?"

"Absolutely. We can have lunch as soon as I've finished my

bunny duties." Yesterday had only gotten better as they settled into their rhythm, like in a game when the team jelled and completed every pass with ease, marching down the field for a goal. And she really wanted to keep playing on Scott's team.

"Very punny." He cringed and stopped at the door that led to the sanctuary. "I can't believe I said that."

"Me, either." She pressed a glove to the door.

"I still can't believe you agreed to this." Chuckling, Scott shook his head. "Ready?"

"Check with Grandma before you open it."

"No need. Who do you think sent me?" He pushed the door. "She said to tell the bunny to hop in as soon as she got here. She did fail to mention that it was you."

"Of course, she did." Rainey skipped the best she could into the sanctuary as the children cheered.

On the playground, Scott stood with the other parents, watching the children run around, collecting eggs. Still in costume, Rainey sat on a bench posing with the kids and their baskets. He needed to get a picture with Henry.

"I found it." Henry waved a golden egg above his head.

"Amazing." Scott squatted, meeting Henry at his level. "What's inside?"

Henry opened the egg and pulled out a gift card. "What is it?"

"It's for an ice-cream sundae."

"It is? Can we go today? Can we take Rainey?" He scanned the crowd. "I don't see her anywhere. I wanted to show her my golden egg."

"Why don't we get a picture with the Easter Bunny, and then I'll help you find her?"

"Okay." Henry dropped the plastic egg into his basket as they made their way to the bench.

Scott gave his phone to one of the teenage girls taking pictures and sat next to Rainey. As he lifted Henry onto his lap with one arm, he found Rainey's gloved hand with the other. It wasn't enough. He wanted to hold her actual hand and tell her how strong his feelings were for her. He wanted this to be the first of many pictures of their trio. His breath hitched. But he needed to give her time to decide. He wouldn't pressure her.

"Smile." The girl held up his phone, snapping the photo. "Y'all are so cute."

"When does the Easter Bunny hop home?" he asked the girl, not wanting Henry to hear Rainey's voice and ruin the effect.

"About five more minutes." The girl took another parent's phone.

"Got it." Scott guided Henry to the playground equipment. He needed a way to buy them some time. "Maybe if you climb high, you'll be able to spot Rainey."

"Yes." Henry passed Scott his basket and dashed across the woodchips. At the top of the play tower, Henry surveyed the area.

Scott's phone vibrated in his pocket, and he retrieved it. *John Allen.* Rainey's dad. Why would he be calling him? Scott answered. "Hello."

"Scott, I'm so glad I caught you. Rainey isn't answering her phone, and I need to talk to her. She needs to report to training tomorrow. Kayce is already on the way."

"But I thought she wasn't coming until tonight. Rainey said she was planning to rest." Even as he said the words, his hope evaporated, leaving him hollow.

"It's a long story. I need to talk it over with Rainey. Is she with you?"

Scott watched the Easter Bunny holding a smiling toddler

with blond curls springing from her head. "She's here, but it'll take a minute for me to get her somewhere she can talk."

"Fine. I'll be waiting for her to call."

"Yes, sir." Scott heard his voice, but it seemed far-off, obscured by the blood pounding in his ears. With his gaze still on Rainey, he could sense the easiness and joy from her, even behind the mask. It was like they were on that beach. Oh, how he wanted to be back by the ocean, where he'd easily ignored all these issues. Everything had seemed new and old at the same time, the possibilities endless, like the expanse of the sea.

"I didn't see her." Henry yanked his basket out of Scott's grasp, almost dragging him over as he ripped him from his thoughts and back to this uncertain reality.

"I'll find her. You go eat lunch with your grandparents." He pointed to the couple sitting at the table they'd claimed earlier.

"But I want to come with you."

Scott turned the little boy to face the tables. "Henry, I need to talk to her alone. Please go."

"Fine." Henry stomped off.

Scott forced his feet to travel the short distance to Rainey's side. Because of the small viewing area in the bunny head, she probably didn't even know he was there.

Rainey passed the little girl to her mother. "She's adorable."

Placing a hand on the bunny's shoulder, Scott crouched by her side and leaned in close to her head. "I need you to come with me."

"Scott?" She turned and squinted through the screen. "Right now?"

"Yes. Your shift is over, anyway. Right?" He checked with the teenage photographer, who gave him a shrug before she wandered away.

"Apparently, it's been five minutes," Rainey laughed.

"Yep." Scott slid his arm under Rainey's elbow and helped her stand, disappointment clenching his heart. They never seemed to have enough time together before they were torn apart. He had resigned himself to their agreement to keep in touch, but he'd also believed that she might be ready to retire. What now?

"Thanks for helping me." She stumbled, but he steadied her as he guided her to the church. "Where are we going? I need to go home and change."

He held the door, pressing his palm to her back. "This is important. It really can't wait."

What did Scott want to tell her? Rainey squinted down the darkened hall as the door clicked shut behind them, and his hand slid around her waist. A wave of excitement swirled through her belly. Or was it fear? How could she feel frightened and delighted at the same time?

Scott guided her into the choir room and closed the door, making her shiver with anticipation. Her breath was so shallow, she was afraid she might pass out. "I—I need to sit." Reaching behind her, she felt for a seat.

"Let me help you." Scott lowered her into a chair. "And now it's safe to take this off." He lifted the bunny head and placed it on the floor.

A rush of heat scorched her skin. "Thanks." Rainey ripped off the fluffy gloves.

"You okay?" Scott sat beside her, resting his arm on the back of her chair. "You look flushed. Do you want me to get you some water?" He brushed a stray hair from her cheek. "It must've been hot in there."

"A little, but it was worth it." All of it was worth it if it ended up with them here together. She'd barely been able to focus after Henry told her that Scott wanted her to stay. Finally, they could talk about it. Rainey glided her hand over Scott's, weaving her fingers with his. "I love being here—" she lifted her gaze to meet his as she leaned into him "—with you."

"Rainey, wait." He inhaled sharply, jerking away from her. "Your dad called." Scott shoved his phone at her. "He needs to talk to you. You need to call him."

"Now?" Her heart hammered. Surely, her dad could wait.

Scott pressed the phone into her palm. "Yes."

"Fine." As she took the phone, Scott trudged to the other side of the room. What was going on? She tapped the screen, calling her dad.

"Rainey?" he answered.

"Yes, Scott said you needed to talk to me." Rainey watched Scott as he pivoted and stalked to the director's stool in the center of the room. He leaned against it, propping one foot on the bottom rung. His eyes slowly drifted from the floor to meet hers.

"I got a call this morning." Her dad's voice sounded excited.

"Okay."

"They are offering you a one-year contract, which is standard."

"Really?"

Scott smiled at her. "Congratulations."

"Yes, but there is a caveat." Dad paused. "They plan to move you from attacking-mid to wingback. I told them you'd play anywhere they wanted."

"But I've hardly ever played that position." She switched her focus from Scott to her thumping white oversize bunny feet.

"You'll be fine. This is your best chance to play." And

maybe her last chance. "Kayce is on her way to Woodley and will drive you to the team training facility tomorrow. They emailed me the contract, and we'll go over it together."

"Okay. Wow. This is not what I expected." She pressed her palm against her thigh, calming her leg. "But I'll be ready when she gets here. Thanks, Dad. Love you." She ended the call with a shaky finger and dropped the phone on the seat beside her.

"So I guess we need to get you home to pack." Scott crossed the room. "It might be easier if you take off the costume first."

"Right." She rocked slightly, her breath shaky as tears pooled in her eyes.

Scott rushed to her side, gathering her under his arm. "Rainey, are you okay?"

"Yes. No. I don't know." She buried her face in his chest. Everything she'd worked for and dreamed of was finally within her reach, so why wasn't she jumping for joy? Why did she feel like she'd been punched in the gut? She sniffled, trying to halt the tears. Surely, these were tears of joy. She was simply nervous about the change of position, and while she'd known if she'd gotten a contract, it would only be for one year, it made her stomach twist.

And she and Scott still hadn't really talked about their relationship. His hand moved gently over her back. Would he wait for her? Could she ask him to?

"Sorry." Rainey lifted her head, wiping the wetness from her cheeks.

"I understand. I may have shed a tear or two when I got called up to play triple A." He released her, moving his arm to the chair. "You'll be great."

"The contract is only for one year. That's standard, so I might be right back here next winter."

"Don't talk like that. You'll be great."

"We'll see. They're making me change positions." She kicked off the bunny feet. "I'll probably just be someone's backup and ride the bench the entire season."

"Rainey, if they didn't want you, they wouldn't have offered you a contract."

"I guess." She reached over her shoulder and tugged down the zipper. The bunny suit fell, pooling around her ankles. "At least I won't be overseas." She stepped out of the costume. Goose bumps covered her skin in the air-conditioned room, but more than that, she felt cold, lonely. She wanted someone objective to discuss her future with. Wasn't Scott supposed to be that person? Turning to face him, she worked her palms over her arms. "If I ask you a question, will you be completely honest with me?"

"That's our arrangement."

"Did you ever consider giving up baseball?"

"Not really." He gripped his knees. "But that isn't my story. Sure, it was my life, but this is my life now, and I'm happy, like I told you on the phone. Don't you want to play?"

"That's always been the plan, but I don't know."

"You've worked so hard for this, and you deserve it. You deserve to live the dream. Where is all this doubt coming from?"

"I don't know." She stacked the parts of the costume on the piano bench. "I guess I'd kind of resigned myself to not making the team, and I had really considered retiring and coaching, and it didn't seem that bad. I actually thought it might be kind of great. Mindy could grow into a dynamic player with the right teacher." She paced the room, avoiding Scott's eyes. It seemed like he thought she should go. Maybe Henry was wrong. "My dad said there's more to life than soccer, and it forced me to open my mind to all the things I'd considered distractions in the past. While I lived here, I got a glimpse of what my life would be like without playing professionally, and I liked it." Stopping at the door, she placed her hand on the handle. "Will you and Henry stop by before you go home? I want to say goodbye."

"Sure. Rainey, this isn't the last play of the last game. It's the beginning of a new season, and you should be excited."

"You're right. I know you're right, and I am excited." She forced a smile. "Promise you'll keep in touch."

"Do you honestly think Henry won't be constantly nagging me to call?"

"True." But they would get busy, and even if they did call, it wasn't the same. She couldn't hug someone over the phone.

Chapter Thirteen

When Scott returned to the picnic, his mom offered him a plate of food, but he had no appetite. Henry had finished a fried chicken leg, a roll, and a serving of macaroni and cheese, but was pushing green beans around on his plate. At least he was acting like a normal kid. The happy chatter of families plucked at Scott's heart. If he'd done the right thing in encouraging Rainey to sign her contract, why did it feel so wrong? He hadn't lied to her, but he hadn't been completely honest. She'd caught him completely off guard, first with the tears and then the doubts. She didn't need him to add to her confusion. She'd thank him when she stepped onto that field and her dreams were realized. It was never easy to leave family and friends, but life was full of hard choices.

"If you don't need us, we're heading home." Scott's mom hugged him. "Your dad needs his afternoon nap. He's already headed to the car."

"Thanks for watching Henry." With his fork, Scott stabbed a couple of green beans and held them up to Henry. "Eat ten beans and then I'll take you to say goodbye to Rainey."

"She's not leaving. I told her you wanted her to stay."

Scott dropped the fork onto Henry's plate. "You what?"

Henry picked at the beans. "I told her you wanted her to stay and be my mom."

"When did you tell her that?"

"This morning before the Palm Sunday parade. Do I still have to eat ten green beans before we go see her?"

"What? Yes." Scott's pulse raced and his gaze swept to the parsonage. Why hadn't she said anything? Or had she? He'd been so intent on encouraging her and not standing in her way, but—

He switched his attention to Henry. "What did she say when you said I wanted her to be your mom?"

"Nothing." Henry shoveled a forkful of green beans into his mouth.

"Nothing?" He squinted at Henry. She'd probably been in a state of shock. He certainly was. It was one thing for them to redefine their relationship, but it was an entirely different thing for him to propose marriage.

Henry swallowed and grinned. "Ten. Let's go. I want to show Rainey my golden egg." He snatched his basket from the picnic bench and sprinted across the field to the parsonage.

"Henry, wait." Scott barreled after the little boy, catching up to him before he darted through the gate. "Rainey made the team, Henry. She just found out, and she's leaving."

"Did you ask her to stay and be my mom?"

"Henry, that isn't how this works."

"Why not?"

"I don't know." Scott massaged the base of his skull. "It just doesn't. I'll explain it all to you when you're older, much older."

Henry shoved the gate. "Grown-ups are so stupid."

"Don't say that word." In one long stride, Scott overtook the boy and crouched in front of him. "Henry, I know this isn't what we wanted, but we need to support Rainey. We support the people we care about. Do you understand?"

"Yes." The little boy's shoulders slumped.

Scott hugged his nephew. "We'll be fine."

"Hmph." Mrs. Ellen stepped around the corner of the house. "I agree with Henry. Don't you want more than fine?"

"Aren't we called to be content?" Scott countered.

"So you were listening in Sunday school, but you've got it wrong. Contentment doesn't equal mediocrity, and it certainly doesn't mean failing to enjoy and use God's gifts."

"God gave Rainey an amazing talent."

"And she's used it to get this far, but can't you see how it led to this moment, to her coming to Woodley just when you'd moved home? The timing seems more than a coincidence. Don't you think? A God-incidence perhaps."

The timing did seem like more than a coincidence, but what if Rainey's time here was only supposed to be for a little while? "God's timing is perfect, but isn't there something about seasons—"

"We don't have time for a theological debate." Mrs. Ellen waved dismissively. "Kayce will be here soon, and at the very least, you need to tell Rainey how you feel. Maybe y'all can withstand a long-distance relationship with enough prayer. You're certainly at the top of lots of prayer lists." She took Henry by the hand. "Scott, you can help Rainey carry her bags to the living room and talk there. We'll be in the kitchen."

If nothing else, he needed to explain Henry's allegations to her. How he would do that after his pleas for honesty in their relationship would be interesting, but maybe—

He searched the sky. "God, please help me find the right words."

As he entered Rainey's room, Scott rapped on the open door. "Need some help?"

Rainey hauled a large suitcase off the bed and turned to face him. A wide navy headband held her hair, revealing her still red-rimmed eyes. A watery sheen covered her slate-blue irises, making them appear like a mountain lake in the early morning. "It has wheels." She rolled it back and forth over the planks of the hardwood floor, the clopping of the wheels echoing in the silent room.

Scott took the luggage handle from her and rolled it out of his way. "Can we talk?"

"I thought we did." She clasped her hands.

"I may not have held up my end of our deal." He crossed the short distance between them, but he didn't dare touch her. Mrs. Ellen might want him to confess his feelings for her granddaughter, but she wouldn't be happy that they weren't in the living room, where she could hear every word. He certainly wouldn't further upset the situation with the caress his fingers itched to make.

"Oh." She pinched her lips, glaring at him.

"I know you know that I wasn't being completely honest. Henry told me, and I'm sorry. I can explain."

Rainey perched rigidly on the edge of the bed. "This should be enlightening."

"Somehow I doubt that." He trekked to the other side of the room and pivoted, grabbing the back of his neck. "You must know that I'd like for you to stay. I've enjoyed our time together, and I'm sure it'd be fun to hang out more, but it's not worth your career. You have an amazing opportunity to live your dream." Slowly, he returned to the spot in front of her. "I want to support you and cheer for you. Not hold you back."

"And the part about being Henry's mom?" she asked a little too calmly, while also scrutinizing him.

"Entirely Henry's idea," he said without flinching. Although he wasn't opposed to the scheme, since Henry had come up with the idea, Scott wasn't lying to her.

"That's what I suspected." She turned up the corners of her mouth and gave a curt nod. "It's for the best. Parents should be with their children, especially Henry. He certainly doesn't need someone flitting in and out of his life. It was no fun when my dad did it to me, and I wouldn't consider subjecting another child to the same treatment." She paused, then waved her hand dismissively. "Not that you asked or anything. We barely know each other."

"I wouldn't go that far, but I do think it's best if we part as friends. Long-distance relationships are hard enough for people who've been committed to each other."

"Of course." Her stoic expression faltered, and she tucked her bottom lip between her teeth. Once again, revealing her doubts over her future.

If she was even considering staying for a possible relationship with him, no matter how likely it was, or how much he wanted it, he'd make sure she understood what a terrible decision staying would be. When he finished, she would stop second-guessing herself. All great players, no matter the sport, innately knew that hesitation during the game always ended in failure.

"Dawn and I'd been together for two years, and when she left, I didn't begrudge her because I didn't want her to resent me later and be bitter about choosing this life that she'd never planned for. And all she was leaving was her job as a Realtor in Pensacola and a carefree lifestyle. It's not like it was her childhood dream to sell houses to military retirees returning to their favorite base."

He met her gaze. "Playing professional soccer is something you've not only dreamed about, but also worked for your entire life. Five years down the road, you might regret your decision when you're watching the team you could've played on win the championship, when you see someone else playing your position, when you hear someone else's name being called over the speakers, when you order a jersey and there isn't one with your name on it. I know how hard it is to give up a dream, and while I've accepted and love my new life, don't think for a second that every so often I don't imagine where I'd be if the accident hadn't happened."

"You're right, but I'll miss y'all, and I'm glad we agreed to keep in touch."

"About that. I think I'm going to need more of a complete break with no contact at least for a while."

"But you said we're friends and we'd keep in touch. What about Henry?"

"I'm not going to deny him his relationship with you, but I need space to reset." How that would work might be complicated, but he'd figure it out later. "Every time we talk or get together, it gets harder and harder for me to say goodbye. Not to mention you need to focus on your game and not worry about carving out time to keep up with me. I don't want you feeling like you owe me a call or to be concerned if days or even weeks go by without contacting me."

"If that's what you want, it's fine, but don't put all of the reasons for this separation on me." She shot to her feet and snatched the handle of her suitcase.

"Rainey, trust me—it's for the best."

"Maybe it is. I get that you're hurting and only part of that has to do with me, so I hope you take the time to heal and do whatever it takes to be sure you can handle a relationship before you drag anyone else into your life."

"You seemed willing to me."

"I did what I needed to do to train. If you'd just agreed to share the field in the first place, none of this—" she motioned between them "—would've happened."

She might as well have kicked him in the gut. How had they gotten here? At least he wouldn't need to worry about her staying for him. At this rate, she may never speak to him again.

"What's going on in here?" Mrs. Ellen appeared in the doorway.

"Nothing apparently," Scott growled.

"Oh, mercy me." Mrs. Ellen splayed a hand over her chest. "Y'all couldn't find the golden egg if the goose laid it on your head."

"Not now, Grandma."

"No time, anyway. Kayce just drove up and Henry's waiting in the living room."

"Good. I'd like to give him a hug and say goodbye." Rainey shoved her suitcase into the hall. "At least I know he loves me," she muttered, but Scott's heart heard her loud and clear, like the opposing team's announcer shouting about a grand slam. It was the ninth inning, and he was too far down in the count to wage a comeback. The game was over.

Swiping away the tears from under her eyes, Rainey could still feel Henry's arms around her as she stared at the closed front door. Scott hadn't even slung an arm around her, he'd just hustled Henry outside. Everything in her wanted to bolt after Scott, but what would she say? Chasing him down wasn't an option. Her heart heaved like she'd just made a breakaway run and was in a face-off with the goalie. Where did she aim her shot? Would she get the goal? Again begging the question, what was her goal?

What?

There was no doubt. She'd attained the goal, and she'd never wavered in her aim to play in the National Women's Soccer League. Not that she needed his approval, but Scott had made it perfectly clear that she should go after it. What right did he have to tell her what to do? The arrogance! What if she wanted to retire? Just because he didn't have the choice didn't mean he knew how she felt.

"Everything alright?" Kayce asked as her hand landed on Rainey's back.

"Fine." Rainey shook her head. "Just tired. It's been a long day."

"Well, we should get going so you can get a good night's sleep."

She doubted she'd get very much sleep regardless of the number of hours she spent lying in bed. Between the nerves swirling in her stomach and the unanswered questions zipping through her brain, the less time in a dark room, the better. Once she was on the field, she could focus on her game and her future.

"We're going to miss you." Grandma approached and gathered Rainey in a hug. "If you change your mind, I hope you know you're always welcome here. Now, don't get me wrong. I'm not saying you should give up your dreams of a professional soccer career. You'll be fantastic, and we'll be cheering you on. But we also love having you close by."

Relenting into the comfort of her grandmother's embrace, Rainey heaved a sigh. "Thanks for all your support. Please give Grandpa a hug for me. I hate that I have to leave in such a rush."

"Of course, honey."

"Please check on Henry." And Scott, but she couldn't give Grandma any hope for the romance. "Make sure he's eating." The boy seemed to be coping better than when she'd arrived. His relationship with his uncle had definitely improved, but when he teared up saying goodbye, her heart grew heavy.

"I'll make him one of your casseroles and drop it by."

"That would be great. And let me know how he's doing with T-ball. He seemed really excited about playing."

Kayce playfully nudged Rainey's side. "I'm sure Scott will keep in touch with you."

"Maybe," she said wistfully. And maybe she'd become a champion square dancer. The chances were about as likely.

Kayce's eyebrows pinched as she regarded Rainey and her grandma. "Did something happen?"

Before either could respond, Rainey's phone rang, and she yanked it from her pocket. "Hello."

"Good afternoon, this is Addison with *Healthy Recipes, Healthy Life*. Is this Rainey Allen?" a bubbly woman asked. Probably a spam call. Next thing she'd be offering Rainey a new set of too-good-to-be-true pans if Rainey attended some demonstration at a hotel. Not a chance, and she didn't have time to let her down politely. She couldn't take any more. Too many emotions collided, assaulting her senses.

She massaged her throbbing head. "Yes, but—"

"Fantastic. You're our first-place winner in the dessert category. Congratulations."

"Excuse me. I'm not sure what you're talking about." She dropped her hand, peering at her grandma.

"You won the recipe contest for best dessert, and I have to say your chocolate banana peanut-butter bites were one of my personal favorites." The woman's high-pitched voice grated on Rainey's fragile nerves.

"I see. Well, thank you."

"We'll be sending an email with all the details. I have your email as Ellen Lorraine at mymail-dot-com. Is that correct?"

"It will work. Thank you." Rainey shoved her phone into her pocket. "Apparently, someone entered one of my recipes in a contest."

"Oh, my stars! And you won." Grandma beamed, her eyes dancing with delight like if she pretended everything was wonderful, her granddaughter might not remember to be irritated.

"Yes." Rainey clenched her jaw.

"I'm not surprised. I love your recipes. I actually thought I'd suggest that if you didn't make the team, you create a blog." Kayce smiled before she saw Rainey's expression.

"I had the same idea." Grandma's excitement waned slightly before she took another tactic and said, "Do you know how many recipe contests there are?"

"No." Rainey shoved down the ire rising in her. Grandma was only trying to help. But did she expect her to quit her soccer career and enter recipe contests? It was ridiculous. Wasn't it? Sure, she'd felt things during her time in Woodley she'd never known she was missing. Things that had changed her. She'd been fulfilled in ways she'd never imagined, but she'd worked her entire life for this opportunity.

Grandma slumped, apparently accepting that Rainey wasn't going to join her in a celebratory dance. "I'm sorry if I overstepped, but when I entered, you didn't know what was going to happen with your tryout. I just thought it'd be something to give you some relief from the pressure, and a different perspective that would help you see other options for your future." Grandma clasped Rainey's shoulders, looking her in the eyes. "But don't think for a second that I wasn't praying for you to make the team, and I'm so glad you did. I'd just hoped that foolish man wouldn't have given up so easily."

"He's probably right." Rainey frowned. "Anyway, we need to go." She rolled her suitcase out the front door.

"Y'all have a safe trip. We'll be praying for you, honey. Don't be a stranger." Grandma waved.

A stranger. Not even a friend. That's what Scott was now. In the matter of only a couple of hours, she'd gone from believing he wanted a long-term relationship with her to absolutely nothing. Rainey settled in the passenger seat of Kayce's car and closed her eyes against the piercing rays of the afternoon sun.

"Do you want to talk about what happened with Scott?" Kayce asked.

"Not now. I'm exhausted. Would it be okay if I rested?"

"Absolutely. Just know I'm here when you're ready to talk."

But what was there to say? Nothing. Scott and Henry lived in Woodley, playing baseball, walking Champ and healing together. She couldn't be a part of their lives, and she needed to accept it.

Chapter Fourteen

Scott slumped against the refrigerator door, hoping something inside would fill the hole inside him, but no amount of food would overcome this empty space. Not that he wasn't willing to try. But he couldn't even gorge himself on junk food because he hadn't bought any since Rainey convinced Henry of the benefits of eating healthy. Scott slammed the door as Henry shuffled behind Champ into the kitchen and slouched onto the floor as the dog munched on his supper. At least someone in the house wasn't fazed by Rainey's departure today.

When he spotted Henry's Easter basket, a ripple of hope poked at Scott's despair. Maybe food was the answer after all. He lifted the golden egg. "Let's get ice-cream sundaes."

"We were supposed to go with Rainey." Henry sulked. "She loves ice cream."

"I know, but she had to leave to join her team tomorrow. We could celebrate in her honor. You can choose her favorite toppings. It'll be just like she's here."

"I don't know her favorites." Henry snatched the egg from Scott and tossed it into the basket. "Besides, if Rainey were here, she'd want us to eat something healthy before having dessert."

"We have one of her casseroles in the freezer. How about

I make one for supper? Then we can go get ice cream." Scott rifled through the foil-wrapped pans, checking the labels for one that would meet Henry's approval.

"It won't be the same." Henry plopped in a chair. "I'm not even hungry. My tummy feels like someone is scraping it out like we did with the pasghetti squash."

Same. Scott banged his head against the top of the freezer. Same. Maybe Rainey was right. Maybe he still hadn't dealt with all his loss and hurt. With her by his side, he'd discovered how good this new life could be. Now what? He had to let go of the crutch that she'd been for him and Henry.

They needed to work through this together. It was time to man up, accept their circumstances and be grateful for the support Rainey had provided, but also know God wouldn't leave them alone. After all He was the great provider, and with this gift card, He was providing a much-needed sugary treat.

Scott slung the freezer door closed. "I know it was hard to say goodbye to Rainey today, but she wouldn't want us to be sad. She'd want us to eat ice cream!" Scott lifted Henry in the air.

"Uncle Scott, you're crazy!" Henry laughed, and Champ jumped around, barking.

"You know it." Scott spun them around one more time before he deposited the boy on a chair. "Get on your shoes. We need to go before they close." Scott checked his phone for the time, but, of course, Rainey's contact came up. He swiped the screen, only to have the picture of them with Rainey in the bunny suit appear. He'd planned to send it to her before he'd declared they shouldn't keep in touch. As bittersweet as the memory was for him, he doubted she'd want it now, anyway.

"Oh, can I see the picture with the Easter Bunny?" Henry tugged on Scott's wrist.

"Sure." Scott gave him the phone.

As Henry studied the picture his smile fell into a frown. "I don't think Rainey even got to meet the Easter Bunny before she left."

"Don't worry about it. I'm sure she's fine." Scott ruffled the boy's hair as he stood. He needed to get Henry back on track and focused on ice cream. "Let's get moving. What toppings are you going to get?"

"Can we please call Rainey and ask her what her favorites are? Please."

"Sorry, buddy. She's busy." Not that he hadn't pulled up her contact every ten minutes since they'd said goodbye, but he'd restrained himself. They needed a clean break. Wasn't there a saying about time healing all wounds? And a couple of hours was no time at all. He rubbed his tight chest. He wouldn't keep Henry from contacting her forever, but today was too soon.

Henry eyed him skeptically. "How do you know?"

"I just do." *Awesome. He sounded just like Dad.* But maybe that was for the best. "I'm going to get your sneakers."

"You don't know anything," Henry mumbled.

"I'm going to get your shoes." Scott strode through the house. Well, that could've gone better, but calling Rainey would only prolong their pain. He had to be the parent. He had to stay firm. If not for Henry, for himself. He'd hated hurting Rainey, but in the moment, it'd felt like the only way. If he'd let down his guard at all, he'd have begged her to stay, and who knew what Henry might blurt out if given the chance to talk to Rainey with everyone so emotional. He couldn't risk his nephew confirming Scott's support of Rainey joining their family. He needed to come up with a plan for Henry to have contact with Rainey that was safe for everyone, and he was too scattered to devise it now.

In Henry's bedroom, Scott grabbed one of the red superhero shoes from the middle of the floor, but the other was nowhere in sight. "Henry, where's your shoe?"

"I dunno," Henry shouted.

Thanks for the help, buddy. Scott dropped to his knees, slid his arm under the bed and retrieved the shoe.

"All righty, here you go." Scott hurried into the kitchen, but Henry was gone. "Henry, buddy, we've got to get a move on. They close in thirty minutes, which is really soon."

"Just a sec. I'm almost done." Henry crouched under the table with Champ.

"Done with what?"

"Nothing."

"But you said—" Scott squatted.

With deep concentration, Henry tapped with precision on Scott's phone. "Dude, you can finish your game later. Give me the phone."

He reached for it, but Henry dodged him. "Not yet." He seriously needed to limit Henry's screen time. The kid was developing an unhealthy attachment to video games.

"Right now." Scott yanked the phone from Henry's grasp. As he rose, he glimpsed the screen, then scrolled through no less than ten rows of emojis. Hearts, dog bones, flowers of every variety, puppies, a little boy, a rainbow, pancakes. "Henry what is this?" A soccer ball, a bunny.

Oh, no.

Slowly Scott checked the top of the screen. Rainy's picture smiled in the small circle.

Henry scurried out from under the table and peered over Scott's arm. "I sent Rainey a text, but I can't spell anything except *Henry*, so I sent pictures." He scrolled through the messages. "I also sent our Easter Bunny picture because I wanted her to see him. Do you think she'll like it?"

No! No! No! Scott gaped at the screen as he collapsed on

a chair. Was there a way to delete a message? His pulse accelerated and he smashed his finger onto the message, highlighting it. The little garbage can appeared at the top of the screen. *Yes!* He tapped the icon. A message popped up letting him know that the action was permanent. *Yes, please.* He confirmed the deletion and watched the pictures disappear. But was it only gone from his device? He'd know soon enough.

Rainey rubbed the sleep from her eyes and stretched her arms and legs out in front of her. She glanced out the window at the city buildings, trying to get her bearings, but with all the recent growth in Jacksonville, not much looked familiar.

"Are we almost there?" She took a sip from her water bottle, relieved the throbbing in her head had subsided during her nap.

"Next exit." Kayce switched lanes.

As they passed a billboard announcing the Jumbo Shrimp's upcoming baseball season, Rainey choked on her water.

"Are you okay?"

Coughing, Rainey cleared her throat and gulped more water. "Yes, sorry, just went down the wrong pipe." But wanting to avoid any further reminders of Scott, she pulled out her phone to check social media. But her notifications indicated two texts from Scott. So much for no contact.

She tapped the screen, and their picture from the egg hunt appeared. Rainey's heart somersaulted. What did it mean? Did she care? She scrolled to the next message, but there were no words, only rows of emojis. *Henry.* She chuckled, but should she respond? She certainly hadn't agreed to not keeping in touch with Henry, and if Scott was letting him use his phone, then he must have consented as well.

Rainey: Assuming your text was from Henry. Please tell him thanks. The picture is great.

Scott: I tried to delete it, but I guess it didn't work. I'll pass on the message to Henry.

Rainey: Thanks.

Scott: He wants to know your favorite sundae toppings.

Rainey: strawberries and chocolate sauce.

Scott: Thanks.

She studied the message chain. What now? Nothing. This was their new normal, and she needed to get used to it.

A new text bubble appeared from Scott.

I hate how we left things. What you said about me needing to heal has been gnawing at me. You're right. I think I confused my feelings about your leaving to play professionally with my own barely scabbed-over wounds from having to retire early. That wasn't fair to you. You should make your own decisions about your life. My advice is clearly tainted. I hope you'll forgive me.

Rainey blinked and reread the message, flexing her fingers.

"Everything okay?" Kayce braked at a stoplight.

Startled, Rainey fumbled the phone. "Yes. It's just a message from Scott. A picture from today. I dressed up as the Easter Bunny." She showed Kayce the picture.

"How sweet is that?"

"Yep. I just need to message him back." She regarded the picture as Kayce continued through the intersection.

Rainey: Of course I forgive you. I'm sorry I said you forced me to coach the kids or spend time with you. It all was fun.

Scott: At least you'll have better memories of Woodley than last time.

Rainey: Truth.

Scott: And if you decide soccer's not your thing, I think you have what it takes to be the Easter Bunny.

Rainey laughed, liking the message. Best to leave the conversation on a high note. She downloaded the picture.

Kayce steered the car into the parking garage for Dad's condo building. His unit was on the twenty-fourth floor of the high rise with amazing views of the St. Johns River.

"Rainey, this is what you want, right?" Kayce tapped Rainey's phone, the picture still on the screen.

"Of course. It's my dream. It's what we planned for and worked for. It's what God made me to do." She closed the app and shoved the device in her bag.

"I'm aware of the plans we've made, but I wouldn't say it's all God made you to do. Just look at the picture. You made a huge difference in their lives." Kayce shut off the car.

"I'm sure they'll find someone else to wear the costume next year." Rainey reached for the door.

"You know that's not what I mean. What about your cooking and coaching? God gave you lots of gifts."

"Are you seriously trying to talk me out of signing my contract?"

"I'm not trying to talk you into or out of anything. I just want to make sure you've thought this through, and it's the right decision for your life now."

"As if I'll have another chance later," Rainey snapped.

"Point taken, but—"

"No." Rainey slumped. "It's been my life's purpose for too long to stop now."

"Maybe it was your purpose for a season of life when you needed it, but it has led you to something very different than you planned. Maybe God has a different purpose for your life. You know He often works this way, and His plans are so much better than ours. Even out of the worst circumstances, God can and does bless us. Look at your dad and me."

"I don't want to disappoint him."

"Your dad only wants you to be happy."

"I know he said that, but—"

"If you don't believe it, you can ask him yourself." She smiled brightly.

Rainey's door opened. "Congratulations! I have a big surprise for you." Dad hugged her before spinning her around. On the other side of the garage, a large red bow set atop a shiny silver Honda Civic.

"You bought me a car?"

"Yep. What can I say? I know your love language isn't gifts, but I have some birthdays to make up for." He held out the key fob with a soccer-ball keychain.

"But how did you get it so quickly?"

"I didn't share your doubts about the tryout. I went to my friend's dealership last week and picked it out. So when we heard the good news this morning, my buddy did me a favor and had it delivered today."

"Wow. Thank you."

"Do you want to check it out?"

"Um, sure." Rainey pressed the unlock button as she approached the car.

Her dad jumped in the passenger seat, while Kayce climbed in the back seat, and Rainey settled behind the steering wheel. As Dad pointed out the features, Rainey's pulse accelerated, her breathing becoming shallow. What was wrong with her? Everything was perfect. Why couldn't she just enjoy it?

"Honey, did you hear me?"

Rainey shook her head, a chill sliding through her. "S-sorry. What?"

"Do you want to take it for a spin?" Dad looked confused and he pressed the back of his hand to her forehead. "Are you sick?"

"No, I don't think so." Although maybe a virus would explain her racing pulse and inability to focus.

"Rainey, I think it's time to tell your dad what we were talking about." Kayce brushed the hair off Rainey's face.

"What's going on, honey?"

After taking several long, deep breaths, she said, "I really appreciate everything you've done for me, and wow, this car is way more than I expected."

"I just want you to be happy, and my actions in the past robbed you of so much joy. This is a small thing." He patted the dash. "But I can't make up for the lost time."

Was she happy? If she'd learned anything from her dad's years of abandonment and recently changed heart, it was not to waste time on the things of this world that wouldn't last. People, family and friends should be at the top of her list of priorities.

Rainey rolled the tiny soccer ball between her fingers. "I'm glad we are working on our relationship."

"Me, too, honey. Was there something else?"

Rainey glanced at Kayce, who gave her a reassuring nod.

"Yes, well, I'm just not certain about my career. How do I know for sure this is the right path for me?"

"Maybe you don't have one-hundred-percent certainty, but what are your concerns?"

"If I pass this up and I make the wrong choice, I can't undo it."

"I mean, that's probably true. What is this really about?"

"My life in Woodley."

"In Woodley?"

"Yes. I love playing on the field, but I really liked coaching the kids, and I won a recipe contest. Grandma and Grandpa are there." Could she change her plans and follow a new direction? This was crazy.

"And Scott." Dad raised his eyebrows.

"Yes, but even though he said he'd like more time with me, he said I should go live my dream, and he needed a clean break."

"And how do you feel about that?" Kayce interjected.

"I don't know. He did apologize when he texted, but he didn't say he wanted to keep in touch beyond what Henry needed." And she couldn't blame Scott.

"It seems like everything was falling into place for you there. You were so happy, and you were miserable at the try-out," Kayce reasoned.

"I wasn't miserable."

"But you weren't happy." Kayce landed her gaze squarely on Rainey.

"I know we've been focused on your career for a long time, and I don't think you've experienced much else." Dad shifted in his seat like he needed more space for whatever he was about to say. He'd always been a pacer in consequential situations, so he likely felt trapped in the small car. Finally, he stilled and said, "I'm sorry for your lack of experiences.

Not to mention the terrible example I've shown of work-life balance or the skewed advice to win at all costs. Unfortunately, I don't think we've ever given you the chance to explore friendships, much less relationships. I just don't want you to regret your decisions."

"When did life get so complicated?" She sighed.

"We're your family, and we want to support you." Dad gathered her hands. "You've had a lot sprung on you and two long weeks of training. Why don't we table this discussion until after you've had something to eat and rested? Then we can weigh your options."

Her options. Home. Family. Why did all those words feel so heavy? She dropped her chin. "I don't know if rest will help."

Her dad squeezed her hands. "Then we'll pray."

"Right now, if you want." Kayce rubbed Rainey's back.

"I'm not even sure what to ask at this point but go ahead." She shrugged. "It can't hurt."

"Lord, our girl needs You," Kayce prayed. "Give her wisdom to know where You want her and help her have the courage to surrender her life to You. We know You only want good for her. Amen."

"Thank you." Rainey's pulse regulated, a measure of peace drifting through her veins. "I sure hope God is clear with His directions."

"Sometimes it's scary to take a step of faith, but no matter where you are, God is there with you. So don't worry about knowing every turn right now, just focus on the path right in front of you," Kayce said.

"Such wise words from my brilliant wife," Dad gushed. "I don't know how I got so blessed to have two such wonderful, strong women in my life, but I'm going to thank Jesus for you every day and do everything I can to be a blessing to you both. Surrendering my will for His and making Him Lord of my life was the best thing I ever did." He gave their hands a firm squeeze before they exited the car.

As Rainey entered the condo, she gazed across the river at the buildings where the Jumbo Shrimp stadium was located. Scott should've been getting ready for the season opener, but he'd been forced to give it all up. Not that she'd ever want the pain and loss that he'd endured, but in the smallest way, she envied his not having to make the choice she faced. Free will always seemed so important until you actually had it.

Surrender wasn't a concept she'd ever relied on. In fact, her usual approach was to exert more energy and take more control. When she played, she never relented, whether winning or losing, until the final whistle blew. She couldn't count the number of times a goal scored in the final minute changed the victor. Still, at this point in her life she felt like she was in a tie game and the overtime period had come to an end. The only thing left was penalty kicks, and she could only control her kick on goal. Then she had no choice but to surrender the results.

Chapter Fifteen

Rainey shuffled into her bedroom, ready for some quiet time away from all the noise that was her past, present and future. But Dad had covered her walls and shelves with awards, medals and pictures of her long relationship with soccer. For most of her life, the sport filled her days, whether it was training at practices, playing games or watching the professional championship series. She'd even read biographies and novels that revolved around soccer players.

While she may not have breathed soccer, it'd been her best friend. The friend she was most herself around. The friend that she could always return to and pick up right with where she left off. The friend that was always present and had been for all her highs and lows. The friend that shared her pain and eliminated her loneliness.

But something in the relationship had shifted. She still loved soccer. If she gave up her dream before playing in the National Women's Soccer League, would all her work and sacrifice have been for nothing?

Rainey's phone rang, and she answered, glad for the distraction from her thoughts.

"Hi, Rainey, this is Angie, Mindy's mom."

What could she possibly want? Rainey lowered on to the corner of her bed. "Hi, how are you? How's Mindy?"

"We're all well, and I hear congratulations are in order for your professional contract."

"Oh, thank you. I start tomorrow." So much for a distraction.

"It seems we were fortunate to have you with us before your career took off. Anyway, I don't want to keep you. I'm calling to first say thank you for helping Scott organize the fundraiser. It is going wonderfully. It looks like we're on track to raise sufficient funds for the field."

"That's great. I know Mindy will be glad. She really took to the game."

"Yes, she's barely without her soccer ball these days, dribbling it around the house, passing it with friends on the playground and convincing her older brother to play goalie in the backyard so she can practice her shots. I've even found her snuggled up with it in bed."

Like her best friend. "Sounds familiar." Rainey scooted across the bed and curled up on her pillows. Out her window, in the last rays of the setting sun, hot pink clouds laced the darkening sky.

"I can imagine, but we do have a problem, which is the other reason I called. We need a coach. I'm sure Scott will do his best in his free time, but I don't imagine there will be much of it, and we'd really like someone with more experience to teach the kids the game. We'd selfishly hoped you might return, but since we obviously wouldn't ask you to give up your career for us, I was hoping you might make some recommendations. Maybe you know someone wanting to move to a small town and start a soccer program from the ground up."

Rainey's heart tumbled, but why? Between her and Kayce, they could help the town find a qualified coach. They'd be fine, probably better off. She was barely a soccer coach as it was, but maybe Kayce was right. Maybe everything she'd learned and experienced was for a different purpose. Coaching Mindy and bringing an effective and engaging soccer program to the kids of Woodley would be something. As her coach, Kayce had been more than something in Rainey's life, she'd been instrumental. Maybe Rainey could be that for Mindy.

"Rainey, you still there?" Angie asked.

"Yes, sorry. I'll talk to my stepmom and we'll come up with someone for you."

"Wonderful. Thank you so much and congratulations again!"

Rainey lowered the phone, closing her eyes. "God, where do You want me? I can see a life in Woodley, but I've always dreamed of playing professionally in the US, maybe even getting called up to the national team. Although last week, I didn't feel like I was with my old friend. It felt lonely and awkward and painful. Still, the pressure to perform and my nerves didn't help, so it might not be the same once I'm a member of the team. But the two short days in Woodley were like coming home. I don't know what to do, Lord, so I'm surrendering it to You. Help me—"

Ka-boom! Boom!

Fireworks? Rainey hustled out of the room in the direction of the sound. "What's the celebration?"

"Jumbo Shrimp game." Dad and Kayce stood at the picture window on the other side of the living room. A shower of lights covered the sky, raining into the river. *Boom.* Purple and pink spirals shot from the stadium.

Was this God's answer? Rainey's eyes filled with tears as her heart trembled for loss, for hope.

"Oh, honey, what is it?" Kayce placed an arm around Rainey, guiding her to the couch.

"I—I think I'm supposed to move to Woodley, but who will I be if I'm not a player?"

"You'll be a child of God." Dad joined them.

"You're right, but it just feels like something inside of me is dying, and it hurts in so many ways, but also it feels like there's something else, maybe even something better."

"It's okay to grieve the loss of a dream, honey. No one ever said retiring from the game would be easy, but we all knew you couldn't play forever. Maybe this is sooner than we'd planned, but that doesn't make it wrong." Kayce dabbed at her own eyes. "I know your heart is breaking right now, and it might ache for a while. Grief is a process and eventually you'll have acceptance."

Another round of fireworks exploded into the dark night, and Rainey focused on the sparkling lights as she released her dreams, allowing room for a new vision. Her heart thudded heavy with the weight of her decision, but at the same time, relief washed through her.

They watched the rest of the show in silence, taking time to process the reality before them. Tomorrow, Rainey wouldn't be driving to the training complex, and while it'd been her decision, they'd allow themselves the freedom to mourn with the faith that God's mercies are new every morning.

With no reason to set her alarm, Rainey let the sunshine wake her. As she blinked open her eyes, she stretched her arms over her head. Wow. She should've tried sleeping late sooner. She felt fantastic. She clasped her hands and prayed God would direct her steps.

After the fireworks show, she'd eaten a somber supper with Kayce and Dad and, feeling emotionally drained, they'd gone to bed early. But as her body awoke, prickles of excitement skipped over her skin. She hopped up and strolled through the condo. Not having anywhere to go or any responsibilities both agitated and calmed her. How was that possible?

"Good morning. I was starting to wonder if you'd get up before lunch." Kayce washed dishes at the kitchen sink.

Rainey checked the oven clock. Ten o'clock. They were already supposed to be at the team's headquarters. "That can't be right. I've never slept past seven and that was only by mistake."

"Well, you had a big day and must've been exhausted. Clearly, your body needed the rest."

"I guess. Where's Dad?"

"He had to go to work, but he asked that you text him and confirm that you are rejecting the offer. He said he could get your arrival time moved to the afternoon, so don't worry about that. We just wanted to be sure you got a good night's sleep. You were pretty emotional yesterday, and we wanted to be sure you wouldn't regret anything once you'd had the chance to think with a well-rested, clear head. This doesn't mean anyone is trying to change your mind."

Certainty expanded in Rainey's chest as she considered her response, then she nodded slowly. "I'll get my phone and text him. If I'd known about this no alarm thing, I may have retired sooner." She nearly skipped to her room. As she returned to the kitchen, she messaged her father and remembered her chat with Angie. "I forgot to tell you last night that one of the moms from Woodley called and asked for recommendations for a coach."

Kayce sliced an avocado onto a piece of whole-grain toast. "Sounds like you've already got a job lined up."

"Is it weird that it's already feeling like a new dream coming true?"

"Not at all." She scraped scrambled eggs from a small cast-iron skillet on top of the avocado and set the plate in front of

Rainey. "And to fuel you for whatever this day holds, a high-protein breakfast."

"Thanks. It's not often someone cooks for me, and it's healthy and delicious." She took a large bite, making sure to get some of all the ingredients.

Rainey's phone buzzed with a text, and she checked it as she continued devouring the breakfast.

I'm guessing you won't get this until after your first training session, but Henry wanted to let you know he's cheering for you and knows you'll be the best. I didn't want to bother you while you were driving and getting settled. We did say a prayer for you, and I hope you make it a point to bask in your dream and really savor every morsel like you do ice-cream sundaes. I really wish I had while I had the chance. Anyway, hope it goes great.

She liked the text, delight and lot of sass flitting through her. "Don't you worry, friend."

"Interesting message?"

"Oops, I didn't mean to say that out loud."

"Your goofy grin would've given you away regardless. I'm guessing it was not your grandmother."

"Ha, no, it was Scott telling me to have a great day and to enjoy living my dreams," she snapped and whisked her finger across the phone screen.

"I see, and you don't agree with him?" She tipped her head to the side.

"Not exactly. You know he's been pretty smug about sending me away like he knows better than me what I want. And I should probably be angry with him, but I know he meant well and really didn't want to stand in the way of me pursuing a professional career."

"That's fair. I'm sure it was hard for him, too. I know we weren't together long, but he really did seem to care for you. And Henry adores you."

"Henry is the best. If it weren't for him, I'd seriously question Scott's feelings for me."

"Why's that?"

"Because Henry's the one who told me that Scott did want me to stay and be his mom."

"What?" Kayce smacked the table. "You could've mentioned that earlier. Way to hide the lead, girl."

"Scott claimed it was all Henry's idea and denied his agreement as he was shoving me out the door to go live my best life, but now, I think it's time to show him just what my dreams look like and how I plan to *savor* them." She chomped another bite. Maybe it was finally time for another batting lesson.

"From the mischief written all over your face, I'm guessing you have a plan."

"Not all the details, but I do know who we should call to help us." Rainey laughed. "Grandma. She'll know just what to do."

Chapter Sixteen

Three games a week didn't leave a lot of time for wallowing, but Scott managed to squeeze it in during his lunch breaks when he was supposed to be watching film for the opposing teams. Never in his life had he been bored by baseball, and he wasn't really now, his mind just refused to stay focused on the details of the game. Of course, the problem might have been the extra hours he'd devoted to preparing for games, trying to avoid his grief. But the results last night had been a win, so he might as well maintain his routine.

Although tonight he had the added distraction of a private batting lesson with a high-school player from a neighboring county. According to the email he'd received from the kid's dad, he'd heard about Scott's career and thought a few lessons with a pro would be good for his son's development. Normally, Scott wouldn't have added anything to his schedule, but for the next couple of weeks, he thought it might be a good idea to fill his evenings when he didn't have games. Less time to give in to temptation and reach out to Rainey.

The bell rang for the next class period, and Scott turned off the monitor and slammed his lunch bag in the trash can. After a busy afternoon of teaching baseball to seventh graders and coaching the varsity practice, Scott met Henry at church for Wednesday night supper. Thankfully, Henry seemed to be coping with Rainey's departure a lot better than his uncle, agreeing to wait until Sunday night to call her because Scott had convinced him that it was best for Rainey.

As Henry finished his cookie, Rainey's grandmother joined them. "We'll be at the house when you finish with the lesson." She'd texted on Monday morning and offered to watch Henry anytime Scott needed help, which had been excellent timing since he'd just read the email from the player's dad.

"Henry, be good for Mrs. Ellen." Scott strode from the social hall to the batting cage and prepared the ball machine for his new student. He wanted to evaluate the guy before he gave any advice.

With a few minutes to spare, Scott grabbed a bat. He positioned himself and swung, breaking the stillness with a satisfactory crack. There was seriously no better therapy than hitting balls. His complete focus zeroed in on the ball making contact at the exact right time in the exact right place. Nothing could break his concentration. He swung again, sending the ball flying to the end of the cage.

"Nice hit." Rainey's voice tripped his nervous breaker, and he nearly slung the bat the way she'd done. He snapped his attention to the entrance.

Rainey moved into the cage, her blond hair glimmering in the light. "So I was sitting in Jacksonville planning the rest of my life and thinking about all the things I'd never learned how to do because of soccer. And I remembered you never finished our batting lesson."

What was she doing here? Had he been set up? Yes, yes, he had, and by the pastor's wife, but what was this? Expectation shot through him, filling his heart, but was he right?

A ball zipped out of the machine, but he dropped the bat by his side. "I can't keep doing this, Rainey."

"Giving me lessons?" She stepped directly in front of him. "Because I'm going to need a lot of coaching."

"I can't keep telling you to leave when it's the last thing I want." He reached down and snatched the power cord. The machine whirred to a whisper.

"I thought we had a deal." She crossed the cage. "But I don't think you've been honest with me."

"And you've been honest with me?" He flipped his gaze to meet hers.

"Maybe not, but I didn't know, and my kissing coach wouldn't give me a second lesson, so I thought I might not be right about my feelings, and I should stick with what I was good at."

Scott drew his finger down the side of her face. "You're beautiful and creative and kind, and you've mastered the art of kissing, and you're a pretty decent soccer player, but it's definitely not all you're good at."

"You know what?"

He shook his head slowly, his heart hammering.

"Even though you still haven't told me the whole truth, I decided I wanted a different kind of future, and I wanted it in Woodley. Apparently, there's a need for someone with my exact set of skills."

"Are you sure?"

"For the first time in my life, I love something more than soccer." She caught her lip in her teeth.

"I really hope you mean me because the whole truth is that I love you and don't want to live without you." He pressed a firm hand to her back.

"Well, that's a relief." Rainey grinned, placing her palm on his chest. "Because I love you and I'm not going anywhere, anymore."

"In that case, do you think we could postpone your batting lesson?" He brushed his thumb across her mouth.

"I suppose we could practice a different skill. You know I'm a perfectionist, and practice does make perfect." She pressed her lips to his, demonstrating her commitment to the drill.

Finally, they were following the same playbook, and with endless time to develop their partnership, they were sure to kick winning goals and hit grand slams—maybe even win a square-dance championship.

Epilogue

Six months later, Scott stood in the school gym with his heart pounding, holding the remote for the sound system. Every day with Rainey had been better than the one before. Together they'd successfully pulled off the first ever Hank and Kristen Wilcox Cooking Competition and Cake Raffle for Woodley Athletics. With the money they raised, they'd completed the first phase of work on the new soccer field, and Rainey's dad had donated goals.

When Rainey wasn't coaching soccer, she worked on her cooking website. Her recipes were a huge hit online, but even a bigger hit with Scott and Henry. Every night before bed, Henry asked her when she could be his mom and move into their house, but Rainey kissed him and Scott good-night and went home to the parsonage, leaving Scott longing for the nights when she wouldn't need to leave. If things went the way he hoped today, he wouldn't have to wait much longer.

Rainey entered the gym and scanned the room. "Scott, Mrs. Mayfield said you needed me in here."

Stepping behind her, he closed the door and pressed play on the remote. Square-dance music blasted from the speakers.

"No way." Rainey spun around, only to smash into him.

He gazed at her, drawing strength from the joy gleaming in

her eyes. "We need to practice." He hooked his arm through hers and danced her in a circle.

"I can think of no reason for us to practice," she laughed.

The music paused and changed to an instrumental version of some swoony love song as the lights dimmed until only the twinkle lights, still up from the middle-school dance, lit the room.

Scott twirled her into his arms.

"This is better." Draping her arms over his shoulders, Rainey snuggled against him as they swayed to the music.

"You know I love you." He kissed the top of her head. "My life before you seems so pointless and shallow, but now, I meet every day wanting to find new ways to love you better."

"You're doing a great job. I love my life with you. It's so much better than anything I ever dreamed of."

Scott stopped moving and stepped back. With his heart thundering louder than the soaring strings, he took Rainey's hands in his and dropped to one knee. "Will you marry me? Will you live our dream together? I love you."

"Yes." Rainey trembled, her beautiful bright smile beating out the tears glistening in her eyes. "I love you. You're the only man I ever want to square-dance with."

* * * * *

Dear Reader,

Who knew being a soccer mom would result in a romance story? Well, of course, God did. I love how He weaves our stories. Until recently, most of my spare time was spent at the soccer fields. When my son started driving himself to practices, I really missed our time together and the thousands of words I used to write during training sessions. Rainey, Scott and Henry's story would not have been possible without the time our family dedicated to the sport, and I wouldn't change anything about it, especially the time with my son.

A huge thank-you to NWSL and USWNT goalkeeper Mandy McGlynn, and her mom, Coach Shannon McGlynn, whom I interviewed. Their insights were invaluable.

My journey to publication has been a long one, but I've seen God work in many ways along the way. I pray you will look for His hand in your own story and remember God works for the good of those who love Him.

Let's stay in touch. Catch up with me on Instagram and Facebook @LeslieDeVooght, and to receive my free novel, *If Only*, join my newsletter at lesliedevooght.com.

Love and Blessings,

Leslie

Get up to 4 Free Books!

We'll send you 2 free books from each series you try PLUS a free Mystery Gift

FREE Value Over **$25**

Both the **Love Inspired*** and **Love Inspired*** Suspense series feature compelling novels filled with inspirational romance, faith, forgiveness and hope.

YES! Please send me 2 FREE novels from the Love Inspired or Love Inspired Suspense series and my FREE gift (gift is worth about $10 retail). After receiving them, if I don't wish to receive any more books, I can return the shipping statement marked "cancel." If I don't cancel, I will receive 6 brand-new Love Inspired Larger-Print books or Love Inspired Suspense Larger-Print books every month and be billed just $7.19 each in the U.S. or $7.99 each in Canada. That is a savings of 20% off the cover price. It's quite a bargain! Shipping and handling is just 50¢ per book in the U.S. and $1.25 per book in Canada.* I understand that accepting the 2 free books and gift places me under no obligation to buy anything. I can always return a shipment and cancel at any time by calling the number below. The free books and gift are mine to keep no matter what I decide.

Choose one: ☐ **Love Inspired Larger-Print** (122/322 BPA G36Y) ☐ **Love Inspired Suspense Larger-Print** (107/307 BPA G36Y) ☐ **Or Try Both!** (122/322 & 107/307 BPA G36Z)

Name (please print)

Address   Apt. #

City   State/Province   Zip/Postal Code

Email: Please check this box ☐ if you would like to receive newsletters and promotional emails from Harlequin Enterprises ULC and its affiliates. You can unsubscribe anytime.

Mail to the **Harlequin Reader Service:**
IN U.S.A.: P.O. Box 1341, Buffalo, NY 14240-8531
IN CANADA: P.O. Box 603, Fort Erie, Ontario L2A 5X3

Want to explore our other series or interested in ebooks? Visit www.ReaderService.com or call 1-800-873-8635.

---

*Terms and prices subject to change without notice. Prices do not include sales taxes, which will be charged (if applicable) based on your state or country of residence. Canadian residents will be charged applicable taxes. Offer not valid in Quebec. This offer is limited to one order per household. Books received may not be as shown. Not valid for current subscribers to the Love Inspired or Love Inspired Suspense series. All orders subject to approval. Credit or debit balances in a customer's account(s) may be offset by any other outstanding balance owed by or to the customer. Please allow 4 to 6 weeks for delivery. Offer available while quantities last.

Your Privacy—Your information is being collected by Harlequin Enterprises ULC, operating as Harlequin Reader Service. For a complete summary of the information we collect, how we use this information and to whom it is disclosed, please visit our privacy notice located at https://corporate.harlequin.com/privacy-notice. Notice to California Residents – Under California law, you have specific rights to control and access your data. For more information on these rights and how to exercise them, visit https://corporate.harlequin.com/california-privacy. For additional information for residents of other U.S. states that provide their residents with certain rights with respect to personal data, visit https://corporate.harlequin.com/other-state-residents-privacy-rights/.

LIRLIS25